Her Dragon Bond

Kia Shadow

Published by Quill & Fury Publishing
Copyright © Quill & Fury Publishing 2024
Website: https://quillandfurypublishing.wordpress.com

Chapter 1

I parked her car at the edge of the tree line and grabbed her notebook and camera from the passenger seat. The rumours of people disappearing in this area of the forest had piqued her curiosity as an investigative journalist. If there was a story here, she wanted to be the one to uncover it.

She slid out of the car and took in her surroundings. The trees were thick on all sides, their branches blocking much of the fading evening light. It gave the woods an ominous feel that raised the hairs on I's arms. Shrugging it off as nerves, she headed down the old dirt path that locals had said may lead to answers.

Her boots crunched on dead leaves and fallen twigs as she walked with purpose but caution. Every so often she would snap a photo or jot down notes about the dense foliage or animal tracks she came across. After about 20 minutes of winding her way deeper in, she spotted something strange hanging from a tree up ahead.

Squinting in the low light, I drew closer and realized it was a wooden sign with a symbol burned into it. It looked like a stylized dragon or serpent wrapped around a flame. She had never seen anything like it before and made a note to research its meaning later.

A rustling sound came from behind her and I whirled around, camera up and ready to snap a photo if needed. But the forest was still and silent once more. Heart pounding, she turned back to the path and continued on with renewed vigilance.

It wasn't long before the trees suddenly opened up to reveal a large, unwelcoming stone structure in the clearing ahead. It looked like an old monastery or castle, with crenelated parapets and towers stretching high into the night sky. Lights flickered in some of the arrow slit windows, suggesting it was still inhabited after all these years.

I crept closer, hugging the tree line for cover, as she surveyed the building. Two massive wooden doors stood closed at the front entrance, with two heavily armed men patrolling back and forth as guards. Whoever or whatever was inside didn't want unwanted visitors, it seemed.

A plan started to form in her mind. If she could sneak in after the guards' shift changed, perhaps she could find clues within to what was really going on here. Her journalist instincts were screaming that this placed held answers to the missing people. But first she needed to wait for nightfall and the cover of darkness.

Crouching low, I made her way around to the side of the structure where the forest grew up right to the stone walls. She pulled out her notebook to record more observations as she waited. Based on the size of the building, she guessed at least 30-40 people could live here comfortably. But why the armed guards and secluded location? What were they hiding?

As twilight deepened into night, I watched through her camera's viewfinder as torchlights bobbed around, signalling the change of the guard. Once all seemed clear, she crept from her hiding spot and cautiously approached one of the windows.

Standing on tip toes, she peered inside but could see only flickering shadows on the stone walls.

Heart pounding with anticipation, I began feeling along the bottom of the wall for any loose stones or other way to gain entry. Her search was cut short by a low, menacing growl from the darkness behind her. Spinning around with a gasp, she came face to face with a hulking figure backlit by the moon.

Glowing eyes the colour of amber regarded her with predatory interest from a beastly face. Muscled limbs ended in vicious looking claws and massive leathery wings folded against its sides. It was like something straight out of a mythical creature book – a dragon in human form.

"What do we have here?" a deep, gravelly voice rumbled from the dragon man's throat. "A little mouse who has wandered into my den. And what business might you have sneaking around my home?"

I tried to steady her shaking voice. "I – I'm a journalist investigating reports of missing people in these woods. This building seemed connected somehow."

The dragon man threw back his head and laughed, a chilling sound that raised the hairs on I's neck. "Curious little thing, aren't you? Well, you've found us dragons now. Though I'm not sure letting you leave is such a good idea..."

4

He took a threatening step closer and I stumbled back until her shoulders hit the stone wall. Trapped with nowhere left to go, she raised her chin defiantly. "I won't cause any trouble, I promise. I just want the truth."

The Dragon Lord regarded her curiously for a long moment before his angular features softened slightly. With the better lighting, as he stepped out of the shadows, I gasped.

His eyes were a dark as my soul, and his teethy grin was a bright as the sun. A contradiction if I ever saw one. Not like myself, with my bright blue eyes, almost piercing; Thanks to my Irish heritage, it was almost impossible for me to tan. But this hulk of a man, who stood towering over me, was something else. I knew in that instant, he was meant to be mine. But first, I had to get out of this pickle I had stumbled into. Whatever story I was working on, I was about to give it a rewrite, and an ending that would rival any best seller. "You have fire in your spirit, I'll give you that. Not many would so boldly walk into a dragon's den." He cocked his head, making a decision. "Very well, you may seek your answers for now. But tread carefully - my kind do not take intruders lightly."

I let out a breath she didn't know she was holding. "Thank you. I promise I mean your people no harm."

With a grunt of what may have been amusement, the dragon man turned and gestured for her to follow. "Come, then. I am Torren, leader of this clan. Let me show you our world, little journalist, before you pass your judgement."

Intrigued in spite of her lingering fear, I fell into step behind Torren as he led me into the stone fortress. Whatever secrets this place held, I was determined to uncover them. My story had just gotten a lot more interesting.

Chapter 2

It was with trepidation that I followed Torren down the dimly lit stone corridor, feeling the hostile stares of the other dragon shifters bearing down on me. Their slitted pupils glowed menacingly in the flickering torchlight as we passed. A few growled low in their throats, making their displeasure at my intrusion known.

Torren paid them no mind, striding purposefully ahead without once looking back to ensure I was still behind him. I tried to ignore the prickling on the back of my neck and concentrate on taking notes of my surroundings. My journalist instincts took over, observing the sparse furnishings and arrow-slit windows looking out over dark forests.

We soon arrived at a massive set of oaken doors, which Torren pushed open to reveal a great hall within. Rusted iron sconces lined the walls, illuminated by the dancing flames within. A long table took up most of the space, with benches on either side. Other doors led off to unseen places further in the depths of the keep.

"You will stay here tonight," Torren rumbled, motioning me inside. "I will have the servants bring you food and furs to sleep by the fire. On the morrow, we will continue our discussion in my solar."

I nodded nervously, clutching my notebook and camera close. "Thank you for your hospitality."

Torren's mouth quirked in what may have passed for a smile on his stern dragon features. "Do not thank me yet, little journalist. My kind are a private folk, and do not take intruders lightly as I said. You have fire in your spirit, but it may yet get you killed here before you find your answers."

With that ominous warning, he spun on his heel and exited, pulling the massive doors firmly shut behind him, leaving me alone in the cavernous hall. I let out a shaky breath and moved to inspect one of the arched windows that lined the outer wall. Peering through into inky blackness, I realized I was already a prisoner here until Torren deemed otherwise.

My journalist curiosity battled with self-preservation instincts, each vying for dominance. This place and its inhabitants held untold secrets, but delving too deeply could cost me my life. I was far outside my realm of comfort and control now. All I could do was cooperate and hope my vulnerability and honesty won me a chance to learn the truth.

As promised, two wary-eyed servant girls soon brought me bread, cheese and wine along with furs to lay by the fire. They scurried away without a word, leaving me to my dinner and thoughts. I ate slowly, meditating on all that had occurred this evening and wondering what new revelations the morrow may bring.

Eventually, exhaustion overtook me and I curled up under the furs, listening to the crackle and pop of the fire and imagining dragons shifting and prowling beyond these walls. Sleep claimed me under a blanket of fear and anticipation for what was to come.

I awoke to the grey light of dawn filtering into the hall through arrow slits high above. Stiff and sore from sleeping on the stone floor, I arose and went to peer outside once more. The forest looked ominously still and quiet. A plume of smoke rose from one of the towers - Torren must already be awake and active in his lair.

Breaking my fast on the remaining bread and cheese, I prepared myself mentally for what was to come. Soon enough, two guards arrived to escort me to Torren's solar as ordered. Clutching my notebook close, I steeled my nerves and followed, determined to get to the truth, whatever it may be, lying in wait behind the dragon lord's door.

The guards led me up winding stone staircases until we arrived at a wooden door guarded by two hulking dragon men. At our approach, they pulled it open with a grunt. I stepped inside, my nerve almost failing me under the cold, calculating stares that turned in my direction.

Torren sat behind a great oak desk, documents and ledgers strewn across its surface. The solar was sparsely furnished but for a few chairs and a roaring fireplace. Tall arrow slits looked out over the misty mountain peaks rising in the distance. He motioned for me to approach. "Come closer, little journalist. Let us continue our discussion."

I nervously complied, very aware of the other dragon shifters in the room regarding me like I was prey. Some wore faces more bestial than human, lips curled back to show fangs even in their shifted forms. Their eyes glinted predatorily.

"This human has no business here," one of them rumbled, a massive brute with jet black scales protruding from his heavy brows. "Send her away before I eat her."

A woman with red hair and wicked curved claws stepped forward as well. "You know our laws, Torren. No outsiders may learn our secrets and live."

Torren held up a hand calmly. "Peace, Ragar, Celise. I have weighed this carefully. The girl's curiosity may yet prove... useful to us. And she came willingly, which is no small thing." He fixed me with a scrutinizing stare. "Now, continue your tale, little mouse. What other questions did you hope to have answered here?"

I took a steadying breath, all too aware of the hostile gazes boring into me. "I came seeking the truth about missing villagers from the area. Are... are they here? Did your kind have something to do with their disappearances?"

Ragar slammed a meaty fist on the desk, making the ink pots rattle. "Insolent girl! You dare accuse us?"

"Enough," Torren said coldly, and Ragar subsided with a growl. "We dragons are a secretive race. But we mean your people no direct harm." He leaned back, steepling his fingers. "The disappearances you refer to were... accidents. Our kind have certain needs that must be met, and not all respond well to our dominance. They were... consumed."

I took notes with a pallid face, struggling to process this new information. Ancient myths of

10

dragons claiming livestock and villagers for food were coming horrifyingly true before my eyes. And yet, Torren spoke so matter-of-factly, as if this was simply their natural way.

"Please," Celise said sweetly, baring her fangs in a mockery of a smile. "Allow me to show the girl to her freedom. This interview bores me."

I began to shake in earnest now, their predatory grins making my blood run cold. But Torren shook his head once more. "She came of her own free will under a banner of truce. No harm will come to her while she is here."

With obvious disappointment, Celise and Ragar backed down reluctantly. But their eyes promised this wasn't over if given the chance. I knew I was walking a razor's edge between life and a most gruesome death. One misstep could seal my fate as these dragons' next meal.

Chapter 3

After my meeting with Torren, I retired to the great hall to collect my thoughts and record my findings so far in my journal. Knowledge was power in this treacherous place, and I hoped to shed more light on the mysterious dragon clan and their secrets.

As I scribbled furiously by the dying fire, movement in my peripheral caught my attention. Two figures slipped into the corridor, glancing furtively over their shoulders as they conversed in hushed tones. I recognized Ragar and Celise, talking animatedly with nervous energy in their postures.

Celise glanced around one final time before discreetly slipping something small into her pocket. My journalist senses were piqued - it seemed I had uncovered an illicit activity right under Torren's nose. Carefully closing my journal, I waited a few moments before rising to follow covertly.

If they caught me eavesdropping, it could mean a deadly confrontation. I had to gather evidence first before confronting them directly. Staying back far enough to avoid detection, I trailed the pair down winding corridors I had not yet explored.

Torches grew sparser the further we went from the noisy great hall, until only dim streaks of sunlight filtering through high arrow slits lit our way. My pulse quickened as we descended a cramped stone staircase into the depths of the keep. Were they leading me to some hidden cache or secret meeting place?

Finally, Ragar stopped before an nondescript wooden door and tested the handle. Finding it unlocked, hc opened it just enough to usher Celise through before following and closing it firmly behind.

I counted to thirty before creeping up and pressing my ear to the crack, hearing only muffled voices within.

Taking a deep breath, I tried the handle tentatively. To my surprise, it turned easily in my hand. Pushing the door open a sliver, I peered inside - and felt my blood run cold. It was no meeting room or storage area...it was a windowless stone cell, pitch black but for a single flaming torch on the wall.

And it was empty.

A creeping sense of dread stole over me as the trap slammed shut behind. I whirled with a gasp to see Ragar and Celise barring the doorway, malice glinting in their feral eyes.

"Well, well, looks like the little mouse wandered right where we wanted," Ragar laughed cruelly. "You were a fool to follow us, girl."

Celise clicked her long nails against the stone wall tauntingly. "Now you'll get to see our...needs up close. Torren won't save you down here."

I backed away till my shoulders hit the cold wall, terror rising like bile in my throat. I had thought myself so clever, investigating clandestine activities, but they had anticipated my journalistic instincts and used them against me. Now I was trapped alone with two bloodthirsty predators without even a window for escape.

"P-Please, I meant your people no harm. Torren said I was under his protection," I pleaded, hating the quaver in my voice.

"Torren is not here," Celise practically purred, savouring my fear. "And we've grown tired of waiting for scraps while that old fool hoards power. A new era is dawning for our kind."

She lunged without further warning, and I threw myself to the side just in time to avoid her slashing claws. Rolling to my feet, I darted for the door only to slam into Ragar's stalwart frame. Massive arms caught me in an unbreakable bear hug as I thrashed and kicked in desperation.

Celise prowled closer, licking her fangs. "My, you are spirited. I think I'll enjoy breaking you."

In that moment, staring imminent death in the face, adrenaline flooded my veins and something primal snapped into place. Throwing my weight backwards with a guttural scream, I head-butted Ragar square in the nose with a sickening crunch.

His grip slackened just long enough for me to wriggle free and dart past a stunned Celise into the corridor beyond. My only thought was to run, run towards the voice of life rather than the yawning silence of my grave. I prayed I could outmanoeuvre two bloodthirsty shifters in their own lair desperate for spilled blood. But if I fell here, at least I went down fighting to the last breath instead of a meal.

My lungs burned as I sprinted through the dark maze of corridors, the heavy footfalls of Ragar and Celise gaining behind me. No matter which twist or turn I took, they seemed to anticipate my movement, herding me further from any signs of life. I knew they were toying with me now, relishing my panic.

As the stone walls blurred around me, a booming roar shook the very foundations of the keep. It echoed with such primal authority that even my pursuers skidded to a halt. I risked a glance over my shoulder to see them backing away slowly, fins laid flat against their skulls in submission.

A massive shadow detached itself from a crossing hallway to block our path. Standing easily over seven feet tall, draconic features melding seamlessly into rippling muscle and gleaming ebony scales, was the most formidable shifter I had yet seen. Heavy wings folded against his back, and a pair of curved ram's horns protruded from his forehead.

Locks of long black hair fell around his chiselled face as he glared down at my would-be killers with eyes that burned like twin infernos. This was no mere clan member - only the raw power and dominance radiating off him in waves could mark him as their leader.

"Torren," Ragar growled respectfully, though a flicker of challenge lurked in his tone. "We caught this girl spying. She seeks to sabotage us from within."

Torren seemed unimpressed by the obvious lie. His gaze raked over me analytically instead, taking in every attribute with calculated interest that made me shudder. As if I was a prize thoroughbred and not a woman running for her life.

"You dare raise your voice in my presence, cur?" he rumbled softly, a threat that carried more weight than any shouted condemnation. "I see only a pair of undisciplined pups who need reminding of their place. Step aside before I beat it into you permanently."

Tail between their legs, Ragar and Celise slunk away without further argument. Only then did Torren turn the full force of his attention onto me, and I struggled not to wilt under the weight of such raw charisma and dominance.

"And you, little mouse. What tale do you have to tell?" I relayed the events as succinctly as possible, omitting no detail in case he detected any lies. His eyes never left mine, capturing me in their mesmeric depths.

When I finished, he gave a rumbling grunt. "So the fates have delivered you unto me after all. Against my every instinct, you are to be my fated mate." Revulsion twisted his stunning features. "Take her to my chambers. She is under my personal guard now."

I could only follow numbly, reeling from this latest shocking development. What cruel joke was this that my life would be forever intertwined with this terrifying yet hypnotic dragon king against both our wishes? Our fates had been sealed it seemed by cosmic forces beyond our control or understanding. All I knew was that my journey had taken a turn into the wholly unknown.

The hours dragged on as I paced my new prison, trapped within the dragon lord's private chambers. Try as I might, I could not escape Torren's piercing stare, watching my every movement like a predator tracking prey.

There was a hunger in his gaze that sent shivers down my spine, though its exact nature remained elusive. Power, control, violence - all lurked barely contained beneath the surface of his flawless façade. I was at the mercy of a force of nature, and one wrong move could unleash my end.

At last, he broke the heavy silence. "You will serve me as my personal maid from this day forth. Clean, mend, fetch - whatever is required without delay or complaint. In return, I vow no harm will come to you under my guard."

It was obey or be thrown to the wolves, literally. Swallowing what little remained of my pride, I nodded stiffly. "As you command, my lord."

My new duties began immediately. I scrubbed then polished armour and weaponry until they gleamed pristinely. Mended tears in lush fox furs and hung them to dry. Prepared food and drink from the well-stocked pantry. All the while, Torren's imperious gaze never left me, evaluating my every motion.

At last, exhausted, I rose from folding the freshly laundered linens to face my master. He crossed the room in two powerful strides, closing the distance between us till I was forced to crane my neck to meet his otherworldly eyes.

Calloused fingers closed around my jaw in an iron grip, tilting my face upward to scrutinize every detail once more. "Do not disappoint me, little mouse. Your life hangs by a thread already. Fail, and you will wish for the mercy of death instead of my wrath."

I shuddered, panicking fluttering in my breast like a caged bird. What more could he possibly demand of me? His warning, though vague, chilled me to the core with its dark implications. Banishment from this dragon's den would surely mean slow torture and death at the claws of his ruthless subjects.

For now, all I could do was nod shakily and pray my skills as a servant proved satisfactory to keep me alive another day in this fortress of fear and tyranny. My future, like my will, was no longer my own to command. All was at the whim of the dragon lord who held my very existence in the palm of his hand.

Chapter 4

I emerged from Torren's chambers weary but determined to complete my tasks, hoping they would help endear me further to my fearsome captor. Little did I know danger still lurked in shadowed halls.

As I descended the stairs, angry voices floated up from below. Peering over the banister, I spied Celise and several other shifters conversing heatedly. Without thinking, I lingered to eavesdrop, journalistic instincts overriding caution.

"Can you believe the audacity?" Celise hissed. "That weak-willed fool actually keeps the human wench as a pet! She should be our evening meal, not wearing our colours."

A scaled brute with tusks laughed harshly. "If she's so special, why isn't she dead already? Our kinds were never meant to mix."

Their discussion turned to mocking tones. "I heard she's Torren's 'fated mate,' can you imagine? A filthy ape mating with royalty! No wonder he seemed offended by the idea."

Footsteps sounded on the stairs and I ducked behind a pillar just in time. Ragar appeared, drawn to the others' merriment. "What gossip have I missed?"

Celise grinned slyly. "Just ridiculing the human's delusions of grandeur. Claims the mighty Torren has chosen her as his bedwarmer, can you believe the gall?"

Her mocking laughter rang out joined by the others, the cruelty of it twisting my gut. I knew then I would never earn their acceptance or trust. To them, I would always be prey - or worse, a joke.

Summoning my courage, I stepped from my hiding place. "You mistake the dragon lord's meaning. He made no claim of affection, only duty to protect what fate has given."

Four pairs of glowing eyes swivelled to fix on me, lips peeling back to reveal glistening fangs. But it was Ragar who spoke, dark amusement lacing his gravelly tone. "Ah, so the little mouse joins our sport! Tell me, how does one preserve fresh meat so long without tasting it?"

"Torren speaks only out of political necessity, nothing more," Celise sneered. "A human mating with royalty? Don't make me laugh. Our kinds haven't mingled in living memory."

I knew then the bitter truth behind Torren's earlier disgust - in their eyes, I could never be considered his equal. My place was below even lowliest servant in their fiercely rigid hierarchy. All I could do was lower my eyes and continue down the stairs, hollow realization crushing what little hope I still clung to in this dragon's den of distrust.

I quickened my pace, eager to escape their jeering whispers still audible behind me. But one comment cut through the laughter, giving me pause.

" If not for Torren's foolish sentiment, that snack would be in our gullets by now. We deserve a leader who puts the hoard first," Celise growled.

My blood ran cold at the rebellious undercurrent in her words. Were they actually considering—

Ragar's harsh tones interrupted my thoughts. "None would dare challenge him. To oppose Torren is to sign your own death warrant."

"Unless..." Celise drew out the word slowly, cunning rippling under her smooth tone. "What if someone else finished the deed for us, anonymously of course? His pet could have...an accident."

Dread pooling in my stomach, I crept closer unseen, pressing into shadowy alcoves to observe unnoticed. A new figure had joined their covert meeting—the massive foreboding shape of Dregan, Torren's most trusted lieutenant.

His raw power rivalled even his master's, yet a subtle unease coloured his movements now as he eyed the conspirators warily. "Tread carefully, whelps. Your scheming will not go unnoticed for long."

Ragar laughed harshly. "Yet you linger still, dragon. What stake have you in preserving the old ways? With Torren gone, a new era could dawn."

Dregan fell silent, contemplating their words as the others watched him sharply for any sign of agreement or betrayal. At long last, he rumbled low, "Your ambition will be the doom of us all if left unchecked. Cease this talk before it festers into treason."

With that ominous warning hanging in the air, he melted back into shadows as quietly as he'd come. The conspirators waited a few tense moments before dispersing reluctantly, shooting dark looks over their scaled shoulders.

I slumped against the wall, mind reeling from what I'd overheard. rebellion was stirring in the folds of the clan and I, as Torren's sworn companion, was directly in the crosshairs of their rising dissent. One misstep could spell a gruesome end at covert claws.

My only choices were to stay silent and pray their scheming went nowhere, or somehow find a way to alert Torren of the threat against his rule without incurring the traitors' deadly wrath. Either path seemed to lead only deeper into danger.

That night as I lay awake worrying over the conversation I had overheard, a shadow passed across the balcony outside my chamber. Quiet as a mouse, I crept closer and peered out into the moonlit wilderness that surrounded the keep.

Down below in the forest clearing, two cloaked figures could be seen meeting in hushed whispers. Even from this height I recognized the bulky frames of Ragar and Celise, no doubt continuing their vile plotting under cover of darkness.

As I watched, a third joined them - the lurking silhouette of Dregan emerging from the treeline. My breath caught in my throat, had he changed his mind and decided to join their insurrection after all?

But the body language was all wrong - Dregan towered over the others with coiled menace, while Ragar and Celise shrank defensively under his glower. Whatever words were exchanged, it was clear the lieutenant was using his vast strength and experience to intimidate, not conspire.

After a few tense moments, the traitors melted resentfully back into the shadows, leaving Dregan alone in the clearing below. His muzzle lifted towards my perch as if sensing eyes upon him. I ducked back just in time, heart racing.

It seemed I had an unexpected ally, if a formidable and inscrutable one, against the rising threat in our midst. Come morning, I would have to find a way to inform Torren of the danger without rousing further dissent. Our lives, and the stability of the entire clan, now hung in the balance. The stakes had never been higher to navigate this den of dragons and survive.

I awoke with a start, disoriented in the pitch black forest. The last thing I remembered was three shadowy figures looming over my bed. Now I was alone.

My pulse quickened as reality set in. They had taken me from the safety of the keep under cover of night. But for what purpose? I sensed no immediate danger, though every snap of a branch made me jump.

Slowly, my night vision adjusted to pick out familiar constellations through the dense canopy. Orienting myself, I began the long trek back towards the mountains in the distance, skirting noisily around anything that moved.

Dawn was just breaking through the trees when I spotted the towering peaks ahead. Exhausted but determined, I picked up the pace. Let them think they had driven me off - I would show them a human was not so easily cowed.

As I crept into the great hall, one scene gave me pause. Celise knelt before Torren's throne, feigning distress. "My lord, I have grave news! In the night, the girl slipped past her guards and fled into the forest. Her fear of you must have driven her mad."

Torren's brow furrowed, clearly troubled by this supposed betrayal of his protection. But then his keen eyes snapped to me, taking in my dishevelled state.

A sneer curled Celise's lip at being caught in her deception. "Impossible...unless she conspired with others to stage this ruse?" Torren rumbled.

Stepping forward, I recounted my abduction in the dark and long journey home. Torren's eyes glittered with a calculating new awareness as he gazed down at Celise. "It seems my clan faces graver threats than a lone human. Return to your post - we will discuss your treachery later."

She scrambled away, shots of panicked loathing flung my way. As for me, I met Torren's heavy stare evenly, a phantom of what might have been respect flickering in his eyes. My stubborn will to survive among these dragons was proving a greater challenge than they had anticipated.

Chapter 5

Torren paced restlessly in his chambers, troubled thoughts weighing heavy on his mind. Ever since the human's narrow escape, whispers of dissent had grown louder among his clan.

More troubling still was the strange bond he felt with the girl. As leader, forming attachments made him vulnerable. Yet he could not deny her presence soothed some inner turmoil he'd long ignored.

Seeking clarity, he observed her from afar. Rather than cower, she carried on her duties with quiet determination. No fragile flower to wilt at the first sign of danger. Her resilience, though unexpected, was admirable.

That night, he summoned her. "Explain why you remain among those who scorn you so." She met his gaze steadily. "To understand is to overcome fear and hatred. If I earn even, one's trust, it is worth the risks."

Her calm wisdom surprised him. Most would flee or cower in her place. "You speak as one well beyond your years. Yet, staying puts target on your back."

"As does your position," she replied gently. "Rulers lead by example, not fear. Show your clan a hand of peace, they may grasp it in time."

Her earnest counsel gave him pause. Had he become so distrusting that even his own people inspired paranoia? A leader who could not lead by inspiring cooperation was no leader at all.

The whispers haunted her no matter where I walked, and all eyes were on me. Not that they made any intention on hiding the fact.

"You'll be food soon enough, human," one shifter hissed. I cleared my throat and tried to pretend I hadn't heard and hastened my pace.

"You can run," he hackled "bur you can't hide."

My heart pounded against my chest. My breath got stuck in my throat. The heels of my shoes taps quickened along the hard flooring. I could feel eyes on me, right until I passed the next corner.

I took a deep breath of relief. How was I going to survive when the shifters only considered me as a walking, talking buffet?

"You shouldn't be out here walking about, alone," a voice called out. I held my breath and turned around to find the Dragon Lord perched on a wall above me.

"How did you…?" I sighed. He flew. Duh! "Nevermind," I grumbled. "What do you want?"

He let out a low chuckle, then leapt down to the ground in front of me. "I was curious. What do you do, when you're not serving me?"

I frowned, trying to work out whether he was serious. I studied the lines on his face, scrutinising his expression. He looked at me, eyebrows raised. "Uh, not much," I sighed. I figured it wouldn't do any harm telling him the truth. "I come back to my room, then sleep. Just like you ordered. What do you think I did in my spare time? Party?"

He scoffed. "No. I just wanted to know. But, since you have to come all the way over to your room and back again, maybe it's time we think about sleeping arrangements."

I blinked. He had only just made me his personal maid. Sleeping there too? This soon? I swallowed hard. It wasn't as if he was unattractive... but, sleeping so close to me? I licked my lips nervously, with no idea how to answer.

"My sleeping arrangements is fine, thank you. But, if I feel the need to move closer, I will tell you... immediately."

He seemed happy with the reply and sauntered away, waving his hand. "Be sure that you do. But I will be keeping a very close eye on you."

I cleared my throat. Of that, I had no doubt.

I woke the next morning with the feeling of anticipation. I had no idea on what I was going to expect over the next coming weeks. The way the dragon lord has been behaving towards me, anything could happen.

I walked out of the room, barely awake.

"Morning," came a greeting.

I turned around, surprised to see someone leaning against the wall outside my door. It was one of the Lord's friends. "Drax," I acknowledged. "What do you want?"

"You're going to work?"

"Yes."

"To the Lord's chambers?"

"Yes," I sighed, and turned to face him. He was smirking. "Do you have a question, or just being nosey?"

"I have been given strict instructions to make sure you arrived… unharmed."

Unharmed. He looked at me, disgusted.

"Why would I be in danger? I'm not a threat."

He was fast and slid in front of me. I halted, almost treading on his toes.

"Whatever spell you have on him, you won't get away with it, witch."

I blinked. "Excuse me?!"

"You heard. Just be thankful you have some time. He wants you alive, for now. But when his real fated mate arrives--whoever it may be, your spell and hold on him will be broken."

I sighed, and was about to rebuke his claims, but he strut off down the hall ahead of me.

The dimly lit corridors of the Dragon Lord's castle filled me with foreboding, as if the shadows themselves whispered ancient secrets. Clutching a basket of fresh eggs and a loaf of bread, I hurried through the labyrinthine passages. Drax, the Dragon

Lord's closest confidant, walked alongside me, his strong presence a comforting reassurance.

We had only just entered the kitchen when the air grew tense, and I sensed a chilling presence approaching. A group of angry dragon shifters materialized from the darkness, their eyes gleaming with a fiery intensity that sent shivers down my spine. The leader, a formidable shifter with scales as dark as night, stepped forward, his voice a low, menacing growl.

" Maxine ," he hissed, "we've warned you before. Leave this place, or suffer the consequences."

My heart quivered with fear, and I instinctively glanced at Drax for support, expecting him to defend me. But to my shock and dismay, Drax stepped back, his eyes averting mine, and he disappeared into the shadows, leaving me alone to face the wrath of the angry shifters.

For a moment, I stood paralyzed, watching Drax's retreating form, disbelief and hurt mingling with my fear. Then, I turned to the menacing dragons, my determination flaring in my eyes.

"I won't leave," I said, my voice shaking but resolute. "This is my home now, and I won't be driven away."

The leader of the shifters bared his fangs, ready to pounce. Just as despair threatened to overtake me, a thunderous roar filled the air. The

Dragon Lord himself, a massive and majestic figure, emerged from the shadows, his scales gleaming like burnished bronze. Drax followed, looking resolute this time.

With a powerful sweep of his wings, the Dragon Lord confronted the would-be attackers. "Enough!" he bellowed, his voice resonating like a powerful incantation. " Maxine stays. This is her home as much as it is mine. Cross her path again, and you'll face the full wrath of this castle."

The other shifters cowered before their formidable leader, recognizing his authority. They slinked back into the shadows, their threats silenced.

I exhaled a breath I didn't realize I had been holding, my eyes fixed on the Dragon Lord, a mix of gratitude and awe in my gaze. The bond between us had just deepened, and I felt a newfound connection to this enigmatic, powerful being.

As the tension dissipated, Drax stepped forward, a shadow of regret in his eyes. He whispered to me, "I'm sorry for what happened earlier. I'll stand by you next time."

I nodded, my heart heavy but resolute. The castle held more mysteries and dangers than I had ever imagined, but I was determined to stay and uncover them all. With the Dragon Lord and Drax at my side, I knew I was meant for something extraordinary in this supernatural world.

As I followed the elder deeper into the castle corridors, I gazed upon the intricate stone carvings that lined the walls. Depicted in vivid detail were tales from the clan's ancient history.

I was drawn to one carving showing winged silhouettes against an auroral dawn. "This marks our ancestors' ascension to the skies as guardians," the elder explained.

His words echoed the meaning I sensed in the carvings - a duty to safeguard nature's balance, not assert sovereignty. I realized how limited my initial understanding of this clan had been.

Floating lanterns illuminated our way with a mystical glow. Their flames danced in hues of purple and blue, as beautiful as the night sky. Runes along the frames hinted at spells for continual growth and renewal, reflecting the dragons' reverence for such things.

Each achievement portrayed was not a show of dominance, but an acknowledgment of our interconnectivity with natural forces. Through cooperation, not conquest, challenges were overcome and knowledge passed to future generations.

As I took in the majestic carvings and profound wisdoms shared, I felt my preconceptions slowly dissolving. This was a civilization deeply spiritual, attuned to forces beyond possession. Here I sensed mysteries that could transform my understanding of humanity itself. I was keen to uncover more of what this place held.

Chapter 6

"What do you mean by that, exactly?" my mate demanded turning to Drax with a frown.

"I... I mean, she is your mate and will be treated with respect until you say otherwise..." Drax muttered, though his cold eyes remained firmly on me.

"As long as I say?" he frowned. He squinted his eyes, scrutinising his friend with a hard glare.

"You sound like the others who consider her food, or was you the one that set it up for her to be... lunch?"

Drax remained silent, and simply bowed his head.

"I will deal with you later," my mate growled. The expression on his face was clear. There would be consequences to his subordinance and any part of the mob that had attacked me earlier.

"She is just your maid," he snipped, still staring at the floor.

"She is my maid, because she is human. Were she a dragon like the rest of us, she would be the fucking queen by now. Do you understand me, Drax?"

His eyes shot up towards him.

"Queen?"

He gave a slight nod. Then, Drax's eyes turned towards me. "Your magic has a firmer hold on him than I suspected. You are very lucky, but soon your luck will run out."

The Dragon Lord stepped between us, his back straightened, and he bulked out his chest. "Excuse me?"

Drax didn't back down this time and looked at him with a steady gaze.

"You are clearly under her spell. But don't worry, I will make sure her hold on you will end. Tonight, you will be freed of her magic."

"There is no magic!" I exclaimed, frustrated.

"I don't believe you."

I rolled my eyes, but my mate had heard enough.

"You have forgotten your place, friend. Perhaps, everyone has. Tomorrow, I will make her my queen regardless, and YOU can be my new maid--along with everyone else who participated in tonight's events."

"But--"

"No! You said your piece. Now you will listen to me."

"She can't be queen!" Drax exclaimed, now ignoring any attempts at being silenced. "Only dragons can be made queen. Humans aren't even allowed on the territory, let alone rule. This is why the gods have made it so the fated mates are dragons."

He raised an eyebrow. "If that's so, then why is this human my fated mate and not one of you?"

"The gods have made a mistake, obviously."

The dragon lord laughed. "The gods don't make mistakes. They make lessons, and clearly, we haven't been listening."

"A lesson? Are you even hearing yourself, my lord?"

"Drax. I think you forget yourself. Perhaps, i should remind you first. You can take her place as my maid, until you have remembered how to act."

"No, no need," Drax replied hurried, taking a step back. "I didn't mean any disrespect. I am just looking out for you, I swear."

He watched him for a moment, before Torren rolled his eyes. "Fine. But so much as a hair is hard on her head, it won't just be me you'll be serving as maid to. Is that understood?"

Drax nodded, bowing to the Lord Torren. "You have my word."

He seemed satisfied with his answer, and then turned his attention back towards me.

"Are you sure you are ok?" he asked me a final time. Three times, I thought to myself. What was this, third time's the charm? "Yes," I stated. "But what are you going to do with the others?"

"Oh, they'll learn their lesson, by witnessing the very thing that they are trying to avoid."

"Getting caught?"

"No. I told you already. I am going to make you queen, and then have you decide whether I should show them any mercy, or have them banished for a time. Your choice."

I thought for a moment. "I suppose, having them serve under me would humble them a little."

"Marvelous suggestion. We'll make the announcement after dinner tonight."

Butterflies in my stomach made my gut turn. How would they react? I had gone from maid to queen in less than two days. If this didn't convince them I was a witch, then nothing would change their minds. Not now, at least.

The halls remained a constant remind that I was never alone. Even with Drax following my every move, the whispers echoed around us.

I continued with my normal duties, not waiting until I was named queen to relax. Though, I was certain there would be some fallout. Since I would be named queen--in name only, I was certain I wouldn't be having any actual responsibility to them all. Though, as times have shown, especially recently, i could be wrong.

The room was a little tidier than normal, though the bed had been slept in, it looked like he had made an effort to make his own bed. I smiled, and tightened the duvet around the mattress, and plumped up his pillow. I moved over to the dresser, watching as i dragged a cloth over the glass. Fingerprints, scattered across the surface, disappeared beneath the fabric and soap. I bent down, picking up the bucket of warm soapy water, sploshing the bubbles over the floor as I walked across the room.

"Watch what you're doing, human!" a voice snapped from behind me. I turned to find one of the shifters, sneering as they reached for the door on my left.

"Apologises," I muttered, trying to get out of the way.

"Apologies?" the woman frowned. She grabbed me by the shoulder and spun me around to face her. She was a pretty woman, with long hair. Though, her face was caked in foundation, and her lipstick had smeared. I could understand the men's attention towards her. Not like myself, who was always considered as someone who was a "plane Jane" as it were. It was very rare for me to wear makeup and even then, it was often worn off before anyone had a chance to see me in it, but other times, no one had noticed.

"Do you think you're better than me?" she demanded. I blinked, realising that she was still scolding me about my clumsiness. What a shock she will get when he declares me as her queen. I held my tongue and muttered my apologies again, before moving into the next room to mop the floor that had been muddied by the dragons' feet.

I racked my brain to try and remember her name. I knew it started with a C. I frowned. Or was it a K? I blinked, suddenly realising that I hadn't been paying attention. It was either Carol or Karen. I couldn't be far off though, right? Music played over the speakers in the communal hall, as a low hum of white noise. I barely acknowledged the tunes that they played. I opened the door and was greeted to another bedroom. His spare, from what I was told. No one really slept in it. I smiled and looked around. The cabinets were a little dusty, but overall, it simply needed a light going over. "What are you doing in here?"

I blinked. Carol, or Karen. Again.

"Just taking a moment to see what needs to be done," I replied curtly.

"Nothing is going to get done with you just standing there. Seriously, what the hell are you sticking around for if you can't do your job right?"

I opened my mouth to retort but decided to keep it shut.

"That's what I thought," she smirked. "He is going to have a field day when I tell him you have been slacking off."

I laughed. I couldn't help it. If only she knew what she was getting herself in for.

"What is so funny?!"

"You tell Lord Torren," I said, putting down my mop. "And then, come back and let me know what he says."

The woman gasped, and raised a hand. Before i knew what was happening, her hand whipped me across the face.

I blinked, as the shock washed over me, stunned. Then, I blinked again. Dead. I thought bitterly, amazed. Aat the gall. When he finds out that she struck me, she was going to be dead.

Chapter 7

I shouldn't have been looking forward to seeing my mate, or to see his rage when he glanced at my red cheeks. It still stung from the slap.

"What happened?" he demanded.

I sighed. "I am sure she will let you know, at any moment now," I replied off-handedly. I pointed towards the woman, whose name I still couldn't remember, as she brushed her hand through her blonde hair and tidied her pleated skirt. Not something I would typically imagine a dragon shifter wearing, but then again, I had nothing to compare my knowledge to. Despite the craziness of the past couple of days, I was still, very much a stranger to these lands, and to the shifters that pulled me in every direction--mostly, to try and have me for lunch.

"Carol," Torren said, calling her over. I smiled, silently congratulating myself on getting her name right.

"Yes, my lord?" she replied back sweetly, sauntering over to his feet.

"You slapped Maxine?"

I watched as she smirked, and then turned her attention back to my mate. "I had no choice," she replied simply. "She was doing a shotty job of cleaning. You're lucky I was there to give her a hand."

His face reddened into a shade, I could only describe as crimson. "Shotty?" he repeated, clearing his throat. I could hear the strained tone in his voice. "What are you talking about?"

"She was standing in the spare room, just looking. Of course, as a maid, I would expect more from her. Otherwise, why would you still tolerate her existence. Seriously, you can thank me later."

"Oh, I wasn't going to thank you," he snapped, snarling at her with disgust. "I am going to skin you, or perhaps, have my mate slap you back and see how you like it."

"Mate?" she asked.

She genuinely looked confused. I almost felt sorry for her. Almost.

"Yes. I have her around because she is my mate, and I have plans for her. Since you're eager to find out what I am going to do with her, let me be the first to introduce you to your new queen."

She turned around to look at the entrance, expecting someone to walk in. Nothing. Her eyes remained on the door. Waiting.

"Who?" she frowned, turning her attention back to Torren.

"My mate."

She blinked, not quite understanding. "Your human mate?"

"Yes."

She laughed. "Oh, that's very funny," she chuckled, breathing a sigh of relief. "I almost took you seriously. So, who's the bride?"

I smirked and stepped beside Torren, who reached for my hand. "Me," I said proudly raising my head. "I am your new queen."

I helped Torren and the new maid Drax prepare for the clan's arrival, setting the great hall with food and drink. As the dragons filed in, their eyes widened at the sight of me, a human, standing beside their lord. Whispers erupted through the hall, confusion and disbelief on their faces.

During the meal, the murmurs grew louder, discontent rippling through the clan. Torren stood, his voice booming as he addressed them. " Maxine is to be my queen." Their reaction was instant. Eruptions of anger and outrage echoed off the stone walls. Some shouted accusations, while others slammed fists on the table. Torren raised a hand to silence them.

"She has proven herself worthy. Maxine is under my protection, and any threat against her will be seen as a threat against me." His stare was icy. "You will show your new queen the respect she deserves."

The hall quieted, though I could still feel the hostility simmering beneath the surface. I stood tall beside Torren, hiding my nerves. I knew convincing the dragons to accept me would not be easy, but with Torren's support, I hoped to someday prove myself their worthy queen.

The silence following Torren's declaration was broken by an angry voice. "This cannot stand! We demand a new Lord be named, and this farce of a mating ended!"

I scanned the hall for the challenger. A powerfully built dragon with ink black scales and piercing amber eyes stared defiantly at Torren.

Torren's voice was icy. "And who makes this demand?"

The dragon stood tall. "I am Trojan Dusk, and I speak for all dragons when I say this human is not fit to be our queen." Murmurs of agreement rippled through the hall.

Torren stared hard at Trojan. "You overstep. Wait outside, and we will discuss this later."

Another dragon jumped to his feet. "Trojan speaks truth! Choose another mate!"

Torren's jaw tightened. "All challengers, outside. I will address you each separately."

Grumbling, the dragons slowly filed out. I moved to speak, but Torren turned away, ignoring me. He reached into a bag beside him and pulled out an ornate crown set with glittering gems. Gently, he placed it on my head.

The clan's silence was deafening. I raised my chin, refusing to show weakness. I hoped Torren knew what he was doing.

I sighed, and then excused myself to the bathroom to splash some water on my face. The bathroom stalls were thankfully, empty. I let out a heavy sigh, shaking my head. Everything was so complicated. I wasn't sure that it was worth it. Would they eat me in the end after all? Was I queen in name only? The Lord Torren hadn't treated me any different than he did when he first saw me. It seemed like months ago now, though in reality, it had only been a mere couple of weeks.

I honestly didn't know how the others would react to me being their new queen. In fact, I was certain they would rebel against it. There were already whispers of overthrowing him. What if they chose a more radical option? These were dragons after all.

"Do you think they'll accept me?" I asked, looking at his face. His expression contrasted to mine. But I knew somehow, they would never accept me. I made a mental note to myself to sleep with one eye open that night. Just case they did try to do something whilst we were vulnerable. Were the heavily armoured guards on our side? Well, his side? I was certain they would turn the other way if it meant getting rid of me.

"It'll be fine," he replied casually. "They know that if they do betray me, it would be the last thing they ever do."

The thought didn't console me, and instead left me with the heavy feeling of dread.

I turned back to the crowd, dragons bellowing in their dismay. "You've gone soft!" they called.

I pressed my lips together into a tight line.

"I think calling me their queen openly like this is asking for trouble," I mutter.

He shrugged, unconcerned.

"We'll cross that bridge when we come to it."

"Look around," I replied with a frown. "We are already there and trying to swim upstream."

"You're worrying over nothing."

I blinked. Red flag much? I glared at him and cleared my throat. "Listen, you may disagree, but I think I am right on this one. You need to tell them something that would soften the blow."

"Like what?" he frowned back at me.

I shrugged. "I don't know. Tell them that it's in name only or something. Tell them that we'll find a way to turn me. *Something* to convince them that I am meant to be here."

I clicked my fingers. "I know! Tell them this."

I whispered my plans into his ear and watched as a smile spread across his face.

"You really think so?" he asked.

I nodded. "Think about it. There hasn't been a human and dragon pairing in centuries. So, by that logic, maybe my dragon side is just dormant. A spell or potion could be the key in waking up my shifter genetics, then they would have nothing to fight you on."

He nodded. "That makes sense."

He turned towards his subjects, all looking back at him with questionable expressions.

"Listen, we were thinking about what you had all been telling us. And maybe, just maybe, you have a point. It *has* been centuries since there was a pairing between the dragons and human as a fated couple. Which means, there has to be some sort of mistake, right? Because, she is clearly my fated mate. No amount of hating is going to change that. It is written. However, what if there wasn't a mistake by the goddess. What if, just maybe, she may be a dragon shifter, like us?"

They called out their disagreements, like there was something to prove.

"Prove it?!" they demanded. "Shift from your human form!"

"That's my point, funny enough," I replied, stepping forward. "What if, instead of there being an error from the gods—since we know they don't make mistakes—what if, there was a problem with me?" I paused to let it sink in for a moment. "What if, I am a dragon shifter, but the dragon side of me has been dominant in my family for some reason. I don't know why, but there had to be a reason to be thinking that I was human, but then, why choose me to be with your dragon lord?"

I could see their quizzical looks try to process what they were being told. It made sense, even if I didn't believe it myself. They begun to mumble. I was hopeful that this was a good sign.

"So then, how would you wake it up?"

I shrugged. "I don't have the answer to that yet. But I will make it my mission to find out, so that I can be the queen you all deserve."

That seemed to have dampened some of their rage. But who the heck would I speak to about shifting? I couldn't very well go to my parents' house about this? Could I? I looked around at the faces of frustration. I didn't look like I had much of a choice.

"I will speak to my elders about the family tree, see if there is a broken link somewhere. Then, a trip to see the healer about restoring my shifter form as it should be."

As I spoke, the faces around me began to soften. I said my piece and went back into the bedroom. I needed some space, and I needed to think. I didn't believe a word of it, but...some of my thoughts from what they were saying, made a degree of sense. But who would break the link to the dragons, and why?

I looked around the room, hoping somewhere that there would be a phone of some sport. He must have been finished with his meeting, and with dinner, as he made his way back towards me. "What are you looking for?" he asked.

I looked at him, leading him down my train of thought. "Well, the thought behind it wasn't completely made up. I do think that somewhere along the line, the link with the dragon side of our family was disconnected. Otherwise, I wouldn't have been chosen to be your mate. Unless, there was a bigger message behind it—other than not being asses to the humans."

He nodded, trying to follow the track I was laying for him. "So, then, I would need to know about my family tree. If there was anyone in the family at some point who was a dragon shifter, and then figure out what changed."

"How can you change something that happened in the future?"

I shrugged. "I don't know. But even in the centuries past, though the bloodline would have been somewhat diluted, there would still be a trace of that DNA in my blood. All I gotta do is find it, and then wake it up somehow."

He sighed. "I am not sure that it would work. I mean, even if there was a slightest bit of a chance that there may have been trace amounts in your genetics, it wouldn't be enough to have you be able to shift."

I nodded. "I'm thinking it was more of an emotional connection rather than a physical one. Think about it, the parings haven't changed in centuries. Which means, that both of my parents would have had to have been dragon shifters as well. The link to our dragons is an emotional link—or psychological. It definitely wouldn't be a physical one, or we wouldn't be mated. Therefore, I need to know what happened, and find out how to reconnect to that side of us."

"And to do that?" he asked, pushing the question I had been struggling with myself.

"I would have to speak to my elders."

"Your parents?"

I shook my head. "No. If she knew about our connection, then she would have told me. Or at least, my mother would. My father… he didn't speak much." I sighed, closing my eyes as I spoke the dreaded words. "I am going to have to speak to my grandparents."

"Why would that be an issue?" he asked with a frown.

I took a deep breath. "They have been somewhat harsh during out last conversation, and things were said."

"Like?"

I shook my head. "Nothing to worry about. I'll deal with it. But I am going to need to make a phone call to make it happen."

He went into the next room and retuned with a phone. "Here," he said quietly. "Make the call."

Chapter 8

I stared at the phone, silently shaking. What the heck was I gonna say?

I cleared my throat and dialled in the number I had memorised too well.

"Hansel speaking. Who's calling please?"

"Hey, it's me," I said, with as much confidence as I could muster.

"What the hell do you want?"

I expected that. "I need a favour."

Hansel laughed hard. "A favour, from me? Why the fuck would I do that?"

I licked my dry lips. This was going to be the hardest thing I had done in my life.

"Because, I need to speak to my grandparents. And they won't do that until we're good."

"Guess you won't be speaking to them then."

"Come on," I sighed. "It's important."

"Tell me."

"It's not of your concern. Please, I just need one favour. Just tell them we're good."

"Lie? You want me to lie? No. If I am gonna bullshit my way through whatever you are going through, then you are going to have to tell me. What is so damn important?"

I groaned. "Fine. I found my fated mate," I said, in the simplest way possible. "But there are... complications."

"Fated mate? Why would you need to speak to our grandparents about that?"

"Because he's a dragon shifter."

"Impossible," he snorted. "There hasn't been a dragon-human pairing for over a hundred years."

"My point exactly. Which means, somewhere along the lines, we have dragon shifter blood. But, I need to know how far back."

"That'd be diluted to shit then. You're wasting your time."

I shook my head. Not that he could see it.

"You're missing the point. Over a hundred years ago, since there was a mixed pairing. Which means, this may not be a mixed pairing—given the goddess don't make mistakes. Ergo, we are also dragon shifters. That leads up to the question, why don't we know about this? What changed? And how do we reconnect to our dragon selves?"

"That's a loaded question. What makes you think she'll know anything?"

"Over a hundred years ago, would put her around HER grandma was alive. Trust me, if something changed in our family, she would definitely know about it."

He sighed, and I could hear him pacing the floors.

"Listen. I can make that call, but I want us to be good, for real. Not just because you need something from me."

I agreed, though I had a feeling this would come at great cost.

"Fine, fine. What is it that I can do for us to be good again?"

"You know what you need to do."

I clenched my jaw. "Something else. You know I won't."

"Not something else. If we are going to be ok again, you need to say it."

"They are just words, for fuck sake! Hansel, give me anything, literally, anything else."

"No. Say it."

I cried out in frustration. It was so stupid. "Fine!" I screamed and held the phone out away from me. "I got beat. Is that what you want to hear from me?! I got my ass beat. He did it. It happened. I do not forgive him. I will never forgive him. I hate him. But nothing I say, declaring it what he did to me, is going to change anything. Nothing will fucking change. So, what good will it do?!"

He was silent for a moment.

"He did what now?"

I spun around. I had completely forgotten that Torren was standing right behind me. I hadn't realised he had stayed. Somewhere in my mind, I had thought he had left the room. And now, he had heard everything. And he looked furious.

"I…uh… it was a long time ago," I muttered, quickly dismissing it as something that happened in the years past. In truth, it hadn't been that long, and it was the reason I couldn't go home again. Not whilst he was still out there, looking and waiting for my return. If I did return. I may not survive to make it back. Especially without my dragon side to fight him off me with.

"Who did what?" he asked again, each word said pointedly in force.

"It's nothing." I replied.

I was still holding the phone. "You need to tell him," Hansel said.

I swallowed hard. Great cost indeed.

"It was someone I knew from childhood. Please, leave it."

"Tell me who it is."

"Tell him," Hansel warned. "Or you won't speak to grandma."

I grit my teeth, forcing the words out of my mouth. It left a bad taste, even to think that I would have to say his name again. "Travis Malone." I grumbled. "Is that better? Do you feel better now?"

"Who is he to you?"

"Nothing," I told him angrily.

"Who was he?"

I licked my lips. These men. Why did they have to interfere?

"My neighbour." I spun around, with tears streaming down my face. "Satisfied? Now you know why I can't go home."

Hansel sighed and cleared his throat before speaking. His tone softer now and cracked a little. "Not really," he said sadly. "But trust me, it helps to get it out in the air. Bottling it up is dangerous, especially for you."

I blinked. "Why especially for me?" I demanded. "I was doing fine forgetting that it ever happened."

He cleared his throat again. He sounded nervous. "What aren't you telling me?"

"Please, don't make me. Not now. It isn't worth it."

"You made me say it. You gotta be open with me as well. This isn't one-sided."

"He… He had plans for you. And the fact that you refused to even acknowledge what he had done to you, gave him a hold over you that no one else had. Because, he believed that you would do *anything* to keep it getting out. That you were damaged goods. And that you would be compliant."

I saw red. I didn't know what I was thinking anymore, or why I said the things I did. I couldn't believe that this was going this way. All I wanted to do was find out what happened years ago, not what happened in my life where it should have been left alone, let the dust bury what he did to me, like it never happened. Not to think he thought he had a hold on me. To think I would be compliant, rather than be viewed as damaged goods? I snapped.

"Damaged goods?" I hissed. "Compliant?" I clenched my jaw and closed my hands into fists.

His face was about to be really compliant when I shove his teeth down his throat.

"It may also have something to do with your dragon connection," he admitted.

I blinked, completely taken off guard. "W-what?"

"Yeah. I know I said about the DNA thing, but if you are right, there is only one reason the dragon bond would be broken."

I thought for a moment, allowing the news to sink in. "What about grandpa?" I asked, thinking for a moment. "Does he know…?"

"About what happened?"

I muttered a "yes" though I didn't want to voice it.

"Yeah. He mentioned something a whilst back. He said that there was a shift, emotionally. A traumatic event, fragmented our psych, so bad, that it blocked the way for any shifter bond to form. He had questions himself, growing up and learned a little about it. It's not something commonly talked about. But it does happen. And the only way to fix that, is to admit what happened to you was out of your control.

You need to heal, and deal with it. Or else, you won't ever get past being stuck. That's what he called it. Stuck. Stuck in one form."

"How do I heal from that?" I asked. "I hadn't accepted anything in recent years. But then, I should have been able to change before that happened."

"You wasn't given the chance to," he replied, casually. "You were hurt before you were of age to transform. That made you stuck. Not many people have that trauma after the change—it's too dangerous."

I swallowed hard. That still didn't explain how I could heal from it, even if it was the source of why I couldn't shift.

"Tell me how," I said.

He let out a long sigh. "You need to speak to grampa. Not grandma. But I will tell them both that we're good, and they can speak freely."

I thanked him and waited for him to call them.

My phone rang almost an hour later. "Hello?" I asked, somewhat nervously.

"It's Hansel," he said. I nodded and waited to hear whether or not things would move alone. I wasn't sure what I would do if they didn't want to see me still.

"What's the damage?" I asked.

"They'll see you," he replied, his voice light. I could almost swear that he was smiling. Not that you can hear smiles over the phone. He sounded happier though.

"They will?" I asked. I wanted to be sure. "When?"

"Tomorrow, at three. You know the park they like to go to?"

"Sure. The one on the other side of the theatre. I can't believe they bought the place."

"Yeah, it took them almost twenty years—and promised them that they can take it back, after they've died, if they put in a tree to remember them by. And the tree, believe it or not, would be planted by the seat where they had first met."

I cleared my throat. Soppy shit really didn't sit well with me. "I can't believe it," I chuckled. "So, I am meeting them in the park? Where about?"

"That's easy," he said with a cheerful tone. "Meet them by the large tree that over looks the duck pond. There's a bench there, and it is well covered for hot days. And on cold days, offers a little shelter from the wind."

"I remember it," I replied. "I'll be there at three. I won't be late."

"Good to know. And you know where I am, when you're ready to come and see me."

I thanked him again and hung up the phone, with Torren watching me with berated breath.

"Well?"

"Well? You heard what the man said. Three o'clock at Maple Park."

"Where's that?" he asked.

I frowned. It hadn't occurred to me that he might not be familiar with it. I thought everyone know of it. I sighed and shrugged my shoulders. "It's on the other side of town, near the sea. But it's fine, it won't take long to get there."

"Great," he said with a smile, and took a step towards me. "I'll take you there myself. It would be nice to see the parents who raised the people who birthed you."

I blinked. "That is a very odd way of saying you want to meet my grandparents," I chuckled. But then again, at what point had any of this been normal. Going by how the day was going, this was just the beginning...

Chapter 9

The next day came much faster than I would have liked. My nerves invaded my body, gripping me to the point where I was unable to breath, let alone move. What if this was a disaster? What if I really was a mere human, and the gods really did make a mistake? What if, I thought with a shudder, someone else was meant to be my mate? I always watched and noted the people around me. The thought it could be one of them—even my neighbour, made me sick to my stomach. I had nothing against them, but none of them really appealed to me. As for my neighbour, he had been hell bent on controlling the village for some time. And I was the first person he had come across that didn't just blindly obey and listened to his threats. I fought back. I told him no. And in the end, it got me, where? He backhanded me so fast, I saw stars. Then, he walked off with his usual swagger, and foretold me, the next time I see him and I don't obey, he would do far worse to me. But I had that score. I stood up to him. I lost, but I stood up to him. I raised my head, just in time to see the pond come into view. When I go back, he will be walking away without his teeth, and without his swagger. That was a promise.

"Maxine?" a woman called out. I could hear the quizzical tone. Not harsh, but uncertain.

"Yeah. Hey ma'. It's good to see you."

My grandfather strayed off towards the water, clutching a bag of torn up bread. He looked back towards me with a little wave, before scattering the bread into the ripples.

"I hear you have some questions," she began.

I held up my hand. "I know, you know what it is about. I mean, is it possible? Could I be a dragon shifter and just not been told about it?"

She sighed, shaking her head. "I always knew this day would come. I always thought it would be your mother to work it out first, but she never considered that she might be a dragon shifter. And she seems to be somewhat acceptance of her human form."

"So was I… until I found my mate and realised that there could be more to my life than I thought. Something more than just existing."

"Yes. You are a dragon shifter."

"So, it's true? The trauma made me stuck?"

She nodded.

I frowned and studied her for a long moment. "Are you a dragon shifter?"

She stared out to her husband. "I was," she said, sighing. She had a far-away look in her eye. I frowned, watching as her eyes glazed over, as though she was watching a past event.

"What happened?"

"Oh. I had trauma of my own," she confessed. "I couldn't deal with mine. But that doesn't mean you can't deal with yours. Yours, you can get past. I am sure of it."

"The neighbour," I stated.

She didn't reply, but simply nodded.

She called over my grandfather, and then exchanged hands. He passed her the bread and looked at me with a sad smile.

"Hello Duck."

"Hey grandpa. Do you know if I can fix my bond with my dragon? It's important."

"Of course, Duck. I wouldn't be here if I didn't know a thing or two about how to fix your situation. Though, it doesn't mean to say, that it'll be easy."

"So, revenge wouldn't be the answer?"

He laughed, hard, and shook his head. "If it was that easy, everyone would be doing it. No. This isn't about pay back, as much as I wish it could be. This is about healing. And how you heal is to take away the power that he had on you. You take it back."

"How? Without revenge, how do I take back whatever hold he had on me?"

He looked at me with his sad eyes and cupped my chin with his fingers.

"You forgive yourself."

It was my turn to laugh, though, he wasn't nearly as amused as I was.

"Oh," I chuckled, "you were serious?"

He nodded. "'fraid so."

"I forgive myself. It couldn't be helped."

"It could be helped," he corrected.

"I don't see how that would help with my healing, Pa."

He thought for a moment and sat down on the bench, overlooking the pond. Grandmother was still feeding the ducks.

"You can forgive him, but he doesn't deserve to be. You forgive yourself. You could have fought back, or at least, ran after him and give it a shot. You could have attacked him when his back was turned, giving you the upper hand. But you didn't. You let him win."

I thought for a moment. "I'm not that kind of person."

"No, you're not. You weren't scared of him or scared that he would beat you again. What were you really afraid of? I know you, and people's opinion has never bothered you."

I thought for a moment. I never really gave it much thought. I just wanted to avoid the drama. I sighed. "I suppose… I was paying him a mercy. If I saw him again, I wouldn't be so reluctant to fight. I'd fight him, and I'd win. But it'd be on my own terms."

He nodded, smiling. "I have seen you knock out bigger men in a less than five hits. How much do you think it'd take to have him on his ass?"

I chuckled. I didn't put much thought into it. "One," I replied, all to readily. "It'd take me one hit."

"So, voice it," he said, "in front of everyone. Make it known. He doesn't hold power over you. You, have power over him. You paid him a mercy, not the other way round."

I sighed. Echoing back his earlier message out loud. "Forgive myself, for letting him get under my skin. So, warn him off, and show him that he doesn't faze me, at all."

"And then, you'll meditate, and reconnect with your dragon." He paused, as if he remembered something, then his eyes lit up. He dug his hand into his pocket, pulling out a teabag. "Oh, and drink this."

"What is it?" I asked, taking it from him. I sniffed it. It smelled sweet.

"Chamomile tea," he replied. "It'll help to relax your mind for when you meditate."

"Meditate?" I asked.

He nodded and smiled. "The mind is constantly busy, and you'll need to clear it of distractions, and focus on what you really want."

That made sense, like the rest of it, I supposed.

"I want to get back connected with my dragon shifter, then I can be with Torren without… complications."

He laughed. He did this a lot. "Complications?" he scoffed and waved his hand. "The only complication is how to make sure that you two stay together. It's not just getting together, it's staying together. It takes work, no matter what the species."

Truth. I didn't consider what would happen after the change. Would they still question me as his mate? What if he decided he didn't want me after all? What if my dragon self was deformed?How would I even communicate with my dragon self?

How would I even communicate with my dragon self? So many questions and suddenly, I was nervous. Suddenly, everything was such a mess. What if I was making a mistake—providing that I was a dragon shifter at all. Times change, things weren't always matched to the species. It could have reverted back to mixed species, and then a couple years down the line, it could change again. I didn't know what was going on anymore, or if I wanted to find out.

"Are you listening?" he asked, frowning.

II blinked, bringing my attention back to my grandfather. "Uh… clear my mind. Got it."

He sighed. A good indication that I had missed something he had said, something important.

"Trust me," he said, shaking his head. "Drink the tea before you meditate."

Chapter 10

I sighed. I guessed, there was nothing more to do. I glanced behind me, where Torren was waiting.

Drax had been watching since we arrived, though, he didn't interfere. I watched as my grandparents walked away, hand in hand. Wishing me luck wasn't necessary, though they wished it any way. I thanked them, still clutching the tea bag in my hand, before sliding it into my pocket.

"Do you know what you got to do?" he asked.

I nodded. "Yeah. Remind that asshole, who he is dealing with." Not that it made the task any easier, I, at least, knew what it was going to take to get my dragon bond to be reconnected. And also, stop the rumours that my neighbour had anything over me. He may try to get the upper hand, but I knew all to well, how it would end. It wouldn't go well for him, that was for sure.

I pointed in the direction of the town center, smiling. "We need to go that way, and head towards the bell tower. That's where my parents live. I'm certain they'll still be there."

"And your neighbours?"

I sighed. "Well, there's only one way to find out, isn't there?"

The roses were dying in the flower beds, and the weeds have since declared wat on the Petunoa's. I expected nothing else of the cleavers. They always managed to find a way to choke out the bigger plants and dominate the garden. Thankfully, it didn't require much force to pull them out. My neighbour would be just as easily removed.

My parents were hanging around the old bakery, on the corner of the town centre. Of course, they were surrounded by friends. I smiled and began to walk towards them.

One… two… thr—

"Oh, my stars! You're alive!" my mother snapped her head round towards me, as her friends pointed in my direction. My parent and their friends rushed towards me, stampeding in my direction, their arms flailing.

"Yes, of course I am," I replied, bracing myself for the hug. "Why wouldn't I be?"

She turned her head towards the houses, clearing her throat. "There was some talk…"

I chuckled. "I don't doubt it. What have people been saying?"

"Not so much people, as in...person," she replied, looking down at the ground.

"I can bet I know who. Let me guess, he thinks he won a fight against a woman, right?"

She nodded. "He has been stating that you're so afraid of him, that you may never come home. And..."

"And... there's more?"

She sighed, shuffling her feet. "It doesn't matter. You're home. Which means, I don't care what he has been saying. It's all lies."

I frowned and held her in my out-stretched arms. "What did he say, mother?"

The pain on her face as her features scrunched up into a scowl. "He says, we should learn from example."

Well, that did it. I blinked at her, stunned.

"Learn from example? I see..."

Her friends huddled in, wanting to interject. "He has been quiet vocal about running the town his way—now that you were out of the picture and telling them their children would be next if they didn't comply."

I took a deep breath. "I see. Well, if it's example he wants. I say, let's give them an example to learn from."

They frowned, as I spoke my next words with deadly intent. "Tell me where he is."

The sun was setting, lighting up the orange sky. Deep red clouds stretched across the horizon. The light provided very little light. But, beyond the cobbled flooring of the street, and the street lights amps that just about works enough, flickered my way to the tower, a distinct voice could be heard, bellowing to the growing crowd ahead of me.

"She bowed down, on her knees. You should do the same. You think you have it so hard? I haven't begun to—"

"Starting your lessons early?" I called out, striding towards him. The crowd fell into a silence, not even the crows would speak. My footsteps echoed the floor, and the eyes of the villagers all darted in my direction.

"Because, I have been hearing that you're keen on them learning by example. Is that right?"

"Uhhh... yes," he said, raising his chin. "I was telling them, how you begged me."

"Oh?" I said, amused. "I didn't realise you were teaching them fiction. My mistake, carry on, then."

"Fiction?" he gasped. He jumped down from his little pedestal stage and bounded towards me. I quietly beckoned Torren to stand back. He was all mine.

"Is it fiction that you were on the floor by my feet?"

"No. That part you got right. But let me refresh your memory of the rest of it." The silence was tangible, and I swear, I could almost hear his heart pounding against his chest. Anticipating, what I would tell his listening audience. I paced towards them, taking it in my stride.

"As I laid there, and you threatened promises of what you would do to me if you ever saw me again, you walked away." I paused. "Did I run after you?"

"No. You were scared!"

I laughed. "Have you looked at yourself lately? I wasn't scared. You should invest in a mirror, because you need a wake-up call and see things as they are, not as what you want to believe."

"I beat you!" he growled. "I hit you so hard, that you were grounded, by my feet."

I smiled. "Yes. And, whilst I was climbing to my feet, let me tell you what I saw. I didn't see a man, walking away as a winner. What I saw was a boy, who was in way above his head. A boy, who had his first taste of violence. A boy, who thought, because I didn't chase you down, that you had won."

I stood in front of his "students", keeping my tone even, and cool. I brushed away a strand of my hair. "You want them to learn a lesson, so here it is. You did not win. I did not give you a win. What I gave you, was mercy. It was my mercy that you were still able to walk away, unharmed. But I knew where you lived. I knew where you worked. I knew what room that you slept. Now, I could have been petty, and set your house on fire and watch you scream. You could have chased after you, and had you begging me for forgiveness for the things you did and said. I could have you pleading for your life, in the hopes that I wouldn't kill your family as you watched. No. Instead, I gave you mercy, and allowed you to walk away with your dignity still attached. But, imagine my surprise when I learn that you had been flaunting your so-called win, and using it to terrorise my friends. So, I am going to do what I should have done and teach you a lesson that you won't so readily forget."

His eyes were wide with terror. His face paled, as I called out his mother. I knew that she was watching. It was her son, and all she could do was watch in despair.

"Marigold," I called sweetly. "Come and join the class, if you may."

The woman, whose hair was thick, black and curly, strode over towards me. I could see she was shaking, as she tried to steady her hands.

"That night," I said with a smile. "Tell him what happened."

She cleared her throat. "You promised," she whispered.

I nodded. "I know. But look what he has done. So, now, you are going to tell him of that night."

"I—I don't remember…"

"Sure, you do. I came and knocked on the door. Your sweet little boy was upstairs in his room, still washing the blood from his shirt. Tell him, what happened whilst he was still wearing my blood."

She looked towards him, as his features hardened. Then turned to me, pleading silently for another act of mercy.

"Tell him," I demanded again. "Or, I will."

She shook, and slowly took a step towards him.

"Son…" she began, her voice shaking, "I—I didn't know, I swear. Not until she told me."

"Told you what?"

I smiled, letting her break the news to him. I wanted to watch his face as the realisation had hit him, of how truly fucked he was.

"I was making everyone some tea, and she excused herself to the rest room…" she began. "After a few minutes, she still hadn't returned, so I followed up the stairs to see what was going on. And… And…"

"And what, mother?" he demanded, though his face was already beginning to lose its colour. He knew what was going to happen next. He remembered that day, and how he boasted… I smiled.

"You were in your room… re-enacting your victory…" she continued. She closed her eyes, looking tired and her voice was heavy with dread. "You were… unclothed and standing at full attention."

"So? My victory made me hard," he announced proudly.

I smirked. "And after your little re-enactment, you went down stairs for a drink. She tried to get you to have a cup of tea, but you had other ideas, no matter how much she insisted that you drink the tea instead."

"So? I deserved that drink."

"Oh, yes. You certainly did. But as you drank that tall glass of ale, not touching the sides as you washed it down with a second after that. You got... sleepy."

"I was exhausted from the win," he argued. "It takes energy, and I used it all."

"Not quiet. I had slipped out by the time you arrived down stairs. But I did say something to your mother on my way out. I told her, to be sure that you drink to celebrate my act of mercy. I had told her, I added a little something, to remind you how...fleeting, victory is."

I paused. "Of course, she was confused. But after, you began to have... trouble, didn't you."

"No!" he scoffed.

I smirked. "Shall I ask the women, instead, about the not-trouble you've been having?"

He stated at me in horror, dreading the implications.

"What did you do to my drink?"

"Oh, just some sleeping pills. But, that's not what I am getting at."

"It can't be worse than that," he snorted. "You didn't need to spike my drink to make me sleep."

"Sleep, no. But to have a deep enough sleep not to notice, yes."

Everyone's eyes followed me, including Torren's, who suddenly couldn't take his eyes off me.

I wasn't always so nice, and I had no trouble of dishing out justice when its deserved.

"I returned to your room that night. You were sleeping soundly. I sprayed a little of my essence on to your pillow."

"So?"

"So. With the daily dose of... me. What do you think is really causing your impotence?"

"You don't mean...?" he struggled getting the words out. His expression twisted into horror and despair.

"That's right," I said, and I walked up to him until I was toe-to-toe with his. "I conditioned your brain into being impotent for every woman you lay with."

I took out a small bottle from my pocket and sprayed it on my neck. Then, turned to hand it to my mate. I strode back to the stairs, grinning. "You have no control over your body, or your mind. And you'll only get hard, for me."

I laughed, and pulled down his pants, for the audience to see. He was fully erect, as he had been that night.

"And the only time you can get it up, you won't be able to use it. Because, I am not yours." I turned to my fated mate. "I am yours."

"My sheets get washed regular. You couldn't do shit to me or my mojo."

I rolled my eyes. "Heightened senses, like a big win, adrenaline, and all the testosterone you were riding that day. It wouldn't matter. With your senses that heightened, it only needed to be for that night. Trust me, that was *all* you were smelling. And you associated that reaction to me. I am the only one your body will listen to. And I am always on your mind. You have won nothing. What I had given you is mercy. I never said the mercy would be pleasant. I could have done a lot worse."

"How?!" he demanded, borderline hysterical. "How could have that been worse?"

I shrugged. "I could have chosen to burn you in your sleep, and watch you scream. But I decided on the less violent approach."

Chapter 11

We sat at the bakery, facing each other. Torren stared at me in disbelief. "What the hell? I mean, why?"

I blinked, trying to think how to put it into words. "I always… had a way with revenge." I said, simplifying it into sounding something lighter than it is.

"But why?"

I smiled. "You mean, why didn't I just kick his ass?" I asked.

He nodded, eagerly waiting for the answer. "Because, it was drilled into me that I must be lady like, and violence solves nothing. Besides, wounds heal and bruises fade over time—and the lessons along with it. My way, is less violent and is a lot more… durable over time, than a couple of punches."

He frowned, unpacking the reality of the situation. "You're really not as timid and vulnerable as you have people believe, are you?"

I shook my head. "I am nice, and I do truly try to look for the best in people. But, don't cross me. I am nice because I choose to be, that doesn't mean it's in my nature."

His eyes widened, as though a dormant memory surfaced. "Wait, there are people—my clan members, that are waiting to be "dealt with", what are you going to do to them?"

I tilted my head. The five of the clan members who had whispered of overthrowing him. I had told him to keep them in a room, and wait for their fate. I smiled.

"Oh, that reminds me," I replied lightly, "did you send those gifts out to their mothers?"

He nodded, frowning. "It's not… mixed in, right?"

I laughed. "Of course not. That would be gross, and I don't want them looking at me like that every time I walk past them. No, nothing that perverse. No, I have something different in store for them. Don't worry about it right now though. First, I need food. I am starving, and then, I think I will do a little meditation."

He looked back at me, as though I had lost my mind. Craziness was subjective though, and I had no intention on letting anyone get the better of me. "If I am going to be their queen, and rule alongside you, I would need to command respect. And Dragons are stubborn, they won't respect anyone unless they are certain it is in their best interest to—and there be consequences if they don't. Fear commands it."

"So, what are the perfumes for?" he asked.

I shrugged. "Because it was a nice thing to do."

He frowned, not believing me. "I don't buy it. Tell me the real reason."

I rolled my eyes. "You're not going to spoil it, are you?"

He shook his head. "No. Tell me."

I sighed. "All right. Assuming that you sent the gift with your well wishes, they would be eager to wear it. They'll see the gift from their lord as a trophy of some kind. And, whilst their sons had been on watch, they are only allowed to be visited by their mothers, per my instructions."

"Yes, but why?"

I smiled. "Mothers have a unique bond with their sons. Mothers are to be respected, whilst fathers set boundaries and challenge them to better themselves. So, with their only visitor being their mothers, the only thing they'll be smelling when they have any interactions, will be their mothers perfume. That perfume smell, will be embedded into their minds and—much like the essence of me—it will condition their tiny brains into associating that scene with their mother. So, after several weeks of being conditioned, we will let them out of their holding cell, and I will be wearing the perfume. I will demand that they apologise of how they disrespected me. And, upon the smell, they will think of their mother. They will comply, and they will apologise as though they had wronged their *own* mothers.

"That won't make them fear you," he said, carefully.

"No. But they have a reputation of being the toughest and most stubborn of your clan—other than you, of course. But, of those who serve you, they are considered the biggest threat. So, if those who are weaker, more reserved members, watch and see those more threatening members bow down and plead for forgiveness, how will it look?"

He thought for a moment. "It's kind of ingenious," he said, thoughtfully. "You're making them think that you're more dangerous than you are."

I smiled. "Oh, no. I am definitely dangerous if I am pushed. But my point is, they'll see how I broke them. And with that thought, the rest of the clan will fall into line. And those few who went against us, will continue to associate me with their mothers because we have the same scent."

"But the scene is fake," he replied, frowning. "It's just perfume. It'll fade, you'll run out, and then what?"

"That perfume is custom made. I spent my teens designing my own perfume. That perfume has my natural scent—just not from the same source as the one I had given to my neighbour. That, needed something a little stronger to take him down."

He watched me in silence, processing what I had told him. "Remind me, not to get on your bad side," he chuckled. I gave him my best smile, and turned to face the row of houses. My neighbour, was still trying to convince his audience that I was full of shit, but none of them were buying it. Slowly, they dismissed him and began to disperse, back to their own houses.

"Looks like the entertainment is over. Let's call it a day. I have a cup of tea to drink, and a dragon bond to fix."

He nodded and rose from his chair.

"If this is what you are like without your dragon, what an earth are you going to be like with it?"

I smiled. "I don't know, but I can't wait to find out."

The expression on his face was more of concerned than excitement. I frowned, perhaps he wasn't ready for me after all. But, only time will tell. And I had a whole new life I wanted to live—and to do that, I was going to be queen.

We walked into the house I was raised and headed into the kitchen at the end of the hall. Everything was how I remembered it, though, in hindsight, it did look a little smaller than I remembered. Had it really been that long? It seemed like it. I switched the kettle on, being sure to ask around to see if anyone else wanted a drink.

They hesitated before declining, though I couldn't see what they were worried about. "Are you sure?" I prompted. "I am making myself a cup, I can make something for the rest of you whilst I am at it."

"No, no. That's quite alright. We'll have something later," my mother stuttered. I rolled my eyes, accepting the answer as a final response. "All right"

I frowned, finished making my food and drink and then went to sit in the lounge. Why was she acting so strange around me? I wondered. I looked and watched as she spoke softly, keeping an eye on Torren. Did she like him? Maybe in the same way I did? No, I told myself. Thar would be ridiculous.

I thought for another moment and watched how she looked at him. For a moment, I caught the look of recognition. They knew each other!

"What's going on?" I asked, putting my plate down on the side, along with my coffee.

"You have been acting like I am about to rip your heads off since we got here. You know, the reason I came back, right?"

She nodded, though she wouldn't look at me. "And I have dealt with the neighbour. So, what else am I missing?"

She cleared her throat and lowered her gaze to the floor. "Nothing," she muttered.

I frowned, not believing her. "Tell me."

She released a heavy sigh and turned towards me, her hands on her hips. "I don't know what you want from me!" she stated, snapping her words. "I haven't seen you in weeks, without no mention of where you were going. And, I have been scared shit that something happened, that *he* had killed you. And yet, here you are as if nothing had happened."

I blinked and looked at her for a long moment.

"I'm fine," I told her. "I was doing a little journalist work and came across his lair. Found out that we're fated mates. Got into a couple of scuffles, over bloodlines, and now we're back and looking to reconnect with myself."

"Reconnect?" she demanded. "There is nothing to reconnect with."

I sighed, heavier than hers had been. All the frustrations of the last couple of weeks stumbled out of me. "We might be dragon shifters, since he is a dragon shifter. I spoke to your parents. They agree. And the reason you haven't shifted, is because something bad happened. You may not remember whatever it was, but bad stuff has kept happening to all of us and prevented us from connecting with our other selves."

My mother looked at me with a lost desperation.

"You're not a dragon shifter," she replied sadly. "None of us are. We haven't been for a long time."

"Meaning what?"

"Meaning, if there is anything there, it isn't going to come back. We don't have a dragon, and nothing bad happened to you."

I almost laughed. "Really? Because *he* happened. I may not be scared of that asshole, but he did enough. And now, I am going to drink my tea and reconnect with my dragon and be Torren's fucking queen."

She shook her head again, sadly, before glancing in the direction of my lord dragon mate. "This won't end well. No amount of meditation and tea will change anything."

"How will you know?"

"Because, I am still human," she muttered. "Trust me. Leave it be and take your relationship as dragon and human. Or don't. But this won't change, and your clan won't accept you."

I couldn't believe what I was hearing! Of all the indignity, I would have thought she would be supportive. I couldn't understand how she had given up. Well, I wasn't about to. I swallowed my sickly-sweet camomile tea and made my way into the bedroom for some silence.

With this much going on, I doubted I'd be able to relax, but my mother didn't raise a quitter, even if she did give up. No matter what the outcome, I was going to be queen.

Chapter 12

The whispers of the voices in the next room seeped through the halls. The quiet mumbling of Torren and my mother. I knew they had recognised each other, and I suspected that her trauma-whatever it may be—was connected somehow. I wasn't sure to what extent, but right now, it wasn't the time to explore what had happened to her.

I sighed and closed my eyes. I could hear my breath, and feel my heart beat against my ribs. I could smell the dust that had settled on the bookshelves to my left, and the Windex from the window on my right. I could feel the soft mattress beneath me, and the lumps of the duvet where it had crumpled on the way in. The air, too, had a scent. I could smell the air freshener my mother had used. It was her favourite, winter pine. It reminded me of Christmas—which was only a couple months away. I paused, the year had passed so quickly this time round. I shook my head, reminding myself to focus. I needed to hear her. I needed to hear the soft whispers of my dragon and shift into who I was meant to become. After a few deep breaths, my body finally begun to relax, and I could, for a moment, see a warm orange glow from behind my eyelids.

BANG!

"What the hell was that?!" I demanded, leaping from my bed and hurrying other to the top of the stairs. My neighbour had kicked in the front door and was looking up at me from the bottom of the stairwell.

"You!" he hissed. "You and me, right now, outside. I am going to fucking teach you and everyone else that no one beats me and gets away with it."

I rolled my eyes, noticing he had his goons with him this time. "Are you sure?" I replied, taking a slow step down towards him. "Because when I reach the bottom, you're going to be digging yourself a grave. A grave, I might add, that you had wished you had crawled into yourself before approaching me tonight."

"I am not afraid of you."

I laughed. "You should be."

He raised his head defiantly. I glanced over to my mother, wondering why she was staring at him. I snapped my head to him looking back at her.

"Did you tell him where I was?" I asked, stunned.

"O-of course not," she replied, stammering.

I couldn't believe her, and I didn't believe the words that was coming out of her mouth.

"You betrayed me?"

I glanced towards Torren, who looked complexed.

"Well?"

He shrugged. "She may have called whilst she was in the bathroom. But I can't say for sure."

I turned towards her. "Why would you do that?"

He smirked, as he stood in front of me. I was almost to the bottom. "She knows it was in her interest."

"Oh?" I asked, tilting my head. "Best interest?" I turned towards my mother, glaring. "I see."

"He was gonna burn us in our sleep," she cried out. "I had no choice."

I sighed. So much violence already. Not that I was complaining. "Fine. If this is what you want, then we'll end it right here once and for all."

"I knew you would see it from my side."

"On the contrary," I told him. "I am barely getting warmed up. Trust me, you'll wish you had stayed away."

He laughed and signalled his goons to approach. Torren stepped in. Beaming. "Nope. This is between you and her. Your friends and stand and watch."

"Not scared, are you?" I asked, taking the last step down.

"Of course not," he bit back.

"Good." I took off my jacket and placed it over the banister. "I am going to make this quick. I want to relax before the day is out."

"You can relax in hell," he hissed. I smiled. "And, tonight, so will you."

I reached for the closest object that I could get my hands on, which just happened to be the most useless thing I could reach. I rolled my eyes. Of course, I couldn't reach for anything that could cause actual damage. But I couldn't care. I had to make it work, even as I began to swing around the Halloween decoration. I raised an eyebrow at my mother. Once again, witnessing as she dragged out the last of the autumn before winter truly hit. The conker on a string. I couldn't believe I was about to use an absolute cliché to put this arsehole on the ground.

"What are you going to do with that?" he demanded, mocking me.

I turned to my mother, watching her expression. "I am trusting that she kept up the tradition of treating the conkers before threading them?"

She nodded, stepping away.

I smiled and looked back at him. "Good. That means, I am going to use this to mess you up. And then, I am going to hang you by this thread. That is what I am going to do." I began to swing the conker, listening to the wind, as it whooshed past my ear. "Remember, you asked for this."

Torren pulled my mother out of the way, as I began to back my neighbour towards the living room, away from most of the breakables.

"I'm sorry!" she cried again, waving her hands. "I didn't know what else to do."

I didn't look at her. She probably was just trying to distract me. I frowned, trying to remember a time when she didn't want me gone. It couldn't have always been like this, could it? I thought hard, racking my brain as hard as I was swinging. Nothing.

"Deceitful," I cried out, flinging the conker towards his face. He moved, but not fast enough, as the conker landed hard against the side of his face.

"Cold," I said again, taking another swing. This time, aiming it squarely at his nose, and missed.

"Witch!" I screamed. Bingo! Blood flew out from his face. He screamed, holding his mouth, and spat out a front tooth.

I turned my attention briefly towards my mother. "Give me one good reason, why I should believe that he threatened you to hand me in, and that you didn't do it to get rid of me!"

My neighbour laughed. "Threaten?" he mocked. "You think I threatened her to turn you in. Actually, it was the opposite. She told me, like before. Make you disappear, or she'll deal with you herself."

I froze. The conker dangled on the end of the string, lifelessly. My own mother betrayed me. And for what? I didn't know and I didn't care. If this was how she wanted me to stay human, then that was her issue. Not mine. I was going to end him, and then I wouldn't return. She will get her wish, knowing that she had betrayed her daughter. And now, everyone knew it.

"How could you mother?" I demanded, tears stinging my eyes. "You were supposed to protect me. Not traumatise me!"

"You're human, and that is all you will be."

I laughed, though it sounded cold even to my own ears. "You can stay in your human form. But I am going to be a lot more than what you will ever be. And I will be loved—not despised and hated or resented. I am done with you—as soon as this arsehole is down. Be thankful you're not joining him."

"You think you're going to beat me again?" he laughed. I held up a finger, signalling him to wait.

"Wh-what is that?" he scoffed.

I turned my attention to him and stepped forward. "I am already done with you. You both deserve each other."

Then, I struck him in the throat. He grabbed his neck, coughing violently, gasping for air. I could see where I had damaged his wind-pipe. Another strike, and he would suffocate, unable to draw breath. I raised my fist, ready to strike him again.

"No," came a voice that I had grown accustomed to.

"What?"

"Don't do it," he said, softly.

"You're joking right?"

"Look at them."

He nodded and pointed towards them. "You see him, right? He's done."

"Done?" I demanded. I glared back at him. "I don't think so."

He pulled me to one side, keeping one eye on the neighbour. "You won't relax whilst you're trying to kill somebody. Leave him. He knows he's lost."

I sighed and gave him a nod. "All right," I muttered. I barely glimpse at him, still unmoving on the floor.

The atmosphere in the air was like static. I couldn't believe that my mother had deliberate stopped me from connecting me with my dragon. Just because she wanted to be more? I closed my eyes, wondering how her parents must have treated her, though think that this was ok. I paused; they were fine about it though… No, no matter how hard I tried to reason it out, it didn't make sense.

The sun shone, though if the tension was visible to the human eye, I would imagine it would look like sparks, or perhaps glitter in the air, hanging around us, attached to our aurora. I sighed, turning back briefly wondering what had become of us.

My neighbour was now awake. He groaned, digging his hands into the dirt, scarping what earth he could grasp under his fingernails.

"P-Please," he whispered. "I-I didn't mean to. Don't leave me here."

I glared at him. My nostrils flared. The indignity of— "You think you deserve my pity? You should have walked away when you had the chance. Come at me again, and I will kill you."

I turned my back again, walking towards the exit of the ever-growing crowd. I was done, and I wanted to be alone to contemplate what my life had become, and what to do with my future. Without my dragon, I would still be no better off than where I was before: Hated and despised by Torren's clan. They would never accept me as his fate without it. So, where would that leave us?

My heart ached. I couldn't believe my own blood would put me in this situation. And my father? Where was he in all of this? I frowned. He hadn't come to see me since I arrived. Was this her doing too? Was he ashamed? Did he know? So many questions, and I had no time to ask any of them.

The hair on the back of my neck stood on end. Something had shifted. I could feel it. I spun around, just in time to see my neighbour, once again, launching towards us. Shifting as he rushed forwards. His claws scrapped at the ground, kicking up dirt in his wake. His scream, running on all fours as his scream turned into a desperate growl of rage. He wasn't a dragon, but it didn't take a genius to see his true form.

I frowned, wondering why he would be so foolish, I may not be a dragon, but Torren certainly was.

Something was off. I frowned, watching his feet. Instinct took over, but I noticed too late. His trajectory changed, and he was no longer aiming at me, but to my fated mate to my left.

"Watch out!" I screamed.

Chapter 13

He spun around, shifting abruptly. He was a natural but wasn't fast enough to move out of the way whilst shifting. My neighbour slammed into him, forcing him to the ground. His head collided with a brick wall. I heard a snap. I whipped my hand to my mouth, mortified, before Torren revealed his broken arm—protecting his head. I breathed a sigh of relief, which quickly turned into anger. I could feel something deep inside of me, welling up with a fury that I had never experienced. Raw emotion, that I had no control over.

I screamed, my feet pounded against the floor. My body twisted and contorted, painlessly, until I was suddenly standing at a stunning ten feet tall, over a meagre five foot six of my neighbour's shifter form.

I let out a roar of intent, before whipping my tail towards him, hurtling him through the air. I caught a glimpse of deep blue scales, that I quickly acknowledged was the colour of my skin. Blue was my favourite colour for as long as I could remember. It made sense that my dragon would be the shade I preferred. At least, it made sense for me. I didn't know enough about how the colours reflected the human form.

I rushed over to my neighbours limbering form and grabbed him by the neck. My claws digging ever so slightly into his flesh. He struggled to break free of my grasp.

"I warned you!" I growled. "I told you to stop. But then you went for my mate! The dragon I love?!"

Torren climbed off the floor, still nursing his broken arm. "It'll heal," he assured me, not taking his eyes from mine. He ignored the struggling small dragon, still fighting for freedom.

"You don't have to do this," he said. "Let him go."

I shook my head. "No. He had his chance to walk away. Now, he'll pay."

He let out a roar of his own. It took less than half a minute before two more dragons landed on the ground beside us. "Hand him to them."

The dragons he had summoned, stood there frowning.

They were a foot shorter than me, and I could tell by their shocked expressions, it wasn't normal.

"What?" I demanded. "Keep staring like that, you'll be in for a real shock."

"Is… Is that you?" the tallest of the two asked.

I rolled my eyes before replying. "We'll discuss this later. Take him now or take him in pieces. I don't care which."

They turned their attention back to my fate mate, the head of the clan. "Take him back now. There's already enough blood shed today."

They nodded, then casted their gaze to his arm.

"It'll heal," he told them, before they had a chance to question it.

With a final nod, they grabbed my neighbour by arms, hauling him off to the sky.

"What an arse," I rolled my eyes again, but feeling a little calmer. Then, turned towards my mate. He looked back at me, grinning.

"You said you love me," he chimed.

I pressed my lips together. "I did… I did say that."

I frowned, suddenly realising that it was the first time I had voiced it out loud.

"You also shifted," he said.

I blinked. I was so caught up, I hadn't had a chance to acknowledge what was going on.

"I did. I shifted!" I cried out. "I'm a dragon!"

He laughed. "Yes, a very large dragon. You really are one of a kind."

I turned towards my mother, still skulking towards the back, ashamed.

"Why didn't you want this for me?" I demanded. "Why would you want this for yourself?"

She sighed and took a small step towards me.

"It's simple. The type of dragons we were… back in the day… we were considered a threat. A freak of nature. I was going to prove to everyone, that we're not to be mocked. We're to be ruled!"

I frowned. "You can't rule a clan without being made the leader. He would never allow that, nor would my father."

She laughed. "Your father is a sweet man. He's no more of a dragon that you were. He doesn't even know what he is."

Bile rose up my throat. "So, you were going to leave him behind, and what? Kill my mate?"

She smirked. "No, of course not. He would be my second in command—after a long day of ruling, a gentle man would be the perfect ending."

He'll find out what he is. And I'll help him be his true self!" I growled. A shadow in the doorway caught my attention. I frowned, taking a step back.

"Thank you, darling, but that would not be necessary."

"Father?"

He walked towards us and shifted into his dragon form. He was almost as tall as I was. His scales were as black as the void and as shiny as chrome. I gasped in awe. "You knew?"

He nodded and turned towards my mother. The corner of his lip curled in disgust. "I am not going to stroke your ego. I am not here to soften your day. No, I am your fated mate. And perhaps you should remember how we met in the first place!"

We all stared in shock. How they met was something they never talked about. I always considered that a little strange. Why wouldn't you want to remember the day you found your true love?

"How *did* you meet?" I asked, intrigued.

"At a meeting," he replied. "Learning about how to connect with our dragons. I never realised that she was trying to learn to disconnect from it. I just always assumed that it was something she disconnected herself."

I shook my head in dismay. "But you knew how to shift? After all this time?"

He nodded again, smiling a sad smile. "Yeah, thanks to your grandparents. They've been helping me reconnect with my dragon."

I was stunned. "I'm glad you found your way," I sighed. Then turned my attention towards mother. "I'm done with your betrayal. You and my neighbour deserve everything you guys have coming your way."

"I'm not a –"

"Yes, you are!" I hissed. And with that, I turned my attention to Torren.

"Let's go home."

He nodded and shrugged out his wings. I watched as his wings stretched out, ready to take off.

Leaping into the air, I thrust myself off the ground, and knew that Torren would be right on my tail.

Back at Torren's home, I closed my eyes to shift back into my human form. I slumped down on the bed, exhausted. "That was exhilarating!" I squealed. "I never knew that flying would be so exciting! I never thought I'd get to experience that… I'm not just a human."

A knock on the door sounded just as he was about to speak. "It's like they know," he chuckled.

He opened the door to find the two guards that had arrived earlier.

"The prisoner is in his cell. Can we talk about…" he frowned, shifting to look towards me. "Was it her?"

Torren laughed. "Yes. She has reconnected with her dragon's bond. And she looked beautiful!"

"I'd never seen a dragon so big!" he gasped.

That would certainly explain the gaping, I thought to myself.

"Yes, well, apparently my mother was under the impression that size matters."

He frowned. "Then she was misinformed. Size has nothing to do with it. The dragons who rule doesn't go by size," he lifted his chin up proudly. "It goes by honour, and loyalty. And the fact that she betrayed you and our kind, shows that she has none. She wouldn't last five minutes here."

I nodded but hesitated before speaking. "And what of me?" I asked. "Are you loyal to me, as you are to your clan leader?"

He bowed. "Yes. And the fact that I mistreated you before, because of your human form, shows that I, too, would not be fit to be a leader. That is why, your fated mate is. He doesn't only see dragons but sees all forms." He paused, looking down a little in disgust. "Not just how they appear…"

"A lesson learned then," I said with a smile. "I learned something too today."

He looked up, frowning. "You have?"

I beamed. "Yes! I learned I am a dragon, I learned that the bond is only as strong as your self-respect, and I learned that I *love* flying!"

He laughed, and then cleared his throat.

"What of the… well, he's no dragon. He has no honour."

I shrugged. "I think he's a hyena."

He nodded. "Hyena shifters are an untrustworthy lot."

He turned towards my mate. "What do you want to do with him?"

He smiled. "Pass him to the lion shifters. They'll have their fun with him."

I cleared my throat. "Sounds like a fitting punishment."

Torren smiled, and pulled me in. "Now, I have business to attend with you."

I blushed, and he held my hand before leading me to a box in the corner of the room. Until now, it had always been locked.

Inside, was a small crown. "My Queen. Would you do the honour of protecting and serving the clan by my side?"

I laughed, wrapping my arms around him.

"Of course, yes!"

He grinned and then moved over to the balcony windows, opening them wide.

"I would like to introduce you to… your new queen!"

The clan members looked up at us, confused and angry.

"She's a human!" they screamed. "You must be jok—"

I shifted into my dragon form, watching as his sentence cut off.

"Uhm…, long live the queen!" he called out.

Chapter 14

I shifted back and laughed. I was finally home.

Torren gazed out his chamber window, lost in thought. Though he'd never admit it, the Queen's bravery intrigued him. Below, she worked tirelessly to gain the others' trust.

That evening, Torren joined the clan for their evening meal. An uneasy truce prevailed as all broke bread together. Only Ragar seemed discontent, glaring daggers at their new ruler.

"My friend, your wrath will only breed more," Dregan told him gently. Ragar growled but said nothing.

As the meal ended, music and dancing began. The Queen watched shyly from the sides. Suddenly, Torren appeared before me. "You claim our ways interest you. Then share in our celebration," he said, offering a hand.

Surprised but willing, I took it. As we danced beneath the stars, barriers seemed to melt away. For the first time, Torren saw me not as prey, but as an equal. His grip softened, and I smiled, wondering if peace between their kinds was possible after all.

I let Torren lead me in the dance, scarcely daring to believe this truce could last. But sure enough, Ragar's resentment grew as the evening deepened.

At last, he hurled his tankard to shatter against the wall. "I'll not stand by as an ape defiles our way of life!" he roared.

All fell silent. Torren withdrew his hand as cool calculation replaced rage in his eyes. "Ape?" He echoed venously. "She is a dragon, and she is your queen!"

Heart in my throat, I appealed to Ragar. "There's been enough blood shed. You don't want to cross me."

"Lies! You must have used magic to shift – you're no real dragon, you're an abomination." Ragar sneered. "You don't belong here."

He grabbed my arm in a crushing grip. I gasped in pain but refused to show further weakness. Torren snarled, "Unhand her, or she'll rip you apart – and you'll be tried for treason with whatever's left of you."

Ragar merely laughed. "Who will enforce it? You? Or are you too soft, like the elder fools before you?"

With shocking speed, he flung me against the jagged stone wall. I heard bones crack but refused to cry out, refusing to give him the satisfaction. Blood welled in my mouth as my vision blurred. I shook my head and prepared to shift – already envisioning his blood on the walls. Torren held a hand out, signalling me to stay put. I frowned but obeyed.

Torren roared in challenge. Fur and scales rippled over his skin as his true form began to emerge. Yet before either could strike, Celise rushed between them, eyes wild.

"Stop, please!" I begged. "We cannot tear each other apart like this. There must be another way."

Ragar sneered down at me. "Surrender the queen, and I'll let her live."

Torren snarled, every muscle taut as a bowstring. I knew that to refuse would mean open war between them, destroying everything the clan had built. Struggling to my feet through a haze of pain, I met Torren's fiery gaze evenly. "Do what you must to keep the peace."

To his credit, shock and regret flickered in Torren's eyes before resolve hardened them once more. He gave me a subtle nod. "So be it. The Queen can leave – but she'll always be your queen, no matter where she is."

Ragar grinned in triumph as Torren helped me stand on shaking legs. "Consider this a lesson to your kind. Stay out of dragon affairs unless you wish to end as a meal."

They escorted me to the gates as dawn broke over the forest. I refused to look back, holding my head high despite the agony raging through my body. At the treeline I paused, meeting Torren's smouldering gaze one last time. Something shifted behind his eyes, a promise I didn't yet understand. Then I turned and limped into the darkness alone.

Days passed in a haze as I struggled through the wilderness. My injuries took their toll, fever raging as infection set in. At last my strength gave out at the edge of a forest pool. As darkness closed in, I saw two golden orbs glowing through the brush...

Chapter 15

My vision faded in and out as the golden eyes drew nearer. Through the haze of fever, I saw scales shifting into a familiar muscled form.

"Torren..." I whispered, choking on the blood in my throat.

He lifted me gently, concern stark against his usual impassiveness. "Keep still. You have a stubborn spirit to survive this far. What did this to you?"

Blackness claimed me then, and when I awoke again, we had returned to the stone fortress. Soft furs cradled me in a chamber lit by crackling fire.

Torren sat vigil, rising when he saw my eyes open. "The fever has broken. Thank the gods."

I tried to rise but fell back weakly. "Why... did you risk coming for me? I thought your kind wanted me gone."

A muscle ticked in his jaw. "I am still leader here. And... as I have told them, you are still the queen, no matter where you go." He paused, as if the words pained him. "You showed the clan that you chose them over your own happiness – though there are a few of them that believe you only left out of self-preservation."

"You should have let me shift. Like I did on the balcony. They would have seen me then."

"Ragar had already told the others his theory that it was a trick. They think you used magic, and that you were vying for power. Though there are some who think you left out of survival – there are those who are still loyal."

His palm, fiercely hot, cupped my cheek. I leaned into its solid comfort without thought. For the first time, I saw past his ferocity to the dragon beneath chained by duty, not cruelty.

"So, you risked your throne to save me?" I asked softly. A rumble rose in his chest, not threatening but intimate in a way no beast's should be.

"Nope. As soon as you left the gate, I had him thrown in the cells. I came back to find you, but you'd already gone." His lips, scorching yet soft, brushed my forehead. "You need to rest now. And then, we're going back home."

The future was filled with paranoia and jealousy; but all that mattered was this moment. Our goals were not so different, it seemed, in longing for home.

I awoke to screams shattering the peace of the keep. Torren was already gone, the blankets still warm from his body. Snatching up my knife, I rushed from the chamber on unsteady legs.

Smoke curled through the hall as shouts and clashes of steel echoed from below. Throwing open the stairs, I glimpsed dragon and hyena forms locked in bloody combat amidst the tables and benches.

A hulking shifter had Torren pinned, raising a jagged blade to end our leader. With a cry, I launched myself at its back, plunging my little knife between its scales. It howled, spinning to fling me off.

Before it could strike, Torren's claws tore out its throat. He pulled me behind him, scanning for new threats. "Your neighbour must have told them about us before we fought earlier."

As if summoned, a heavily armoured beast burst into the hall, followed by two more. Their hide was craggy and scarred, eyes wild with bloodlust under no command but their own.

"Scavengers!" Torren snarled. He shoved me behind an overturned table. "Stay down and survive."

Then he launched himself at the intruders with claws and fangs bared. Though wounded, his fury was a terrible thing to witness. But three against one can only end once.

Teeth and talons closed around Torren's throat. With a strangled cry he fell, blood pumping from horrific wounds.

NO! A wordless scream ripped from my lungs as I flung myself at the killers, shifting into my dragon form. I grabbed hold of the intruders, flying them into the air and then driving them back into the ground, again and again. Their bones snapped and crunched beneath me, into a bloody mess. Mortified, they released my mate and set their fear-filled eyes on me.

The hall fell silent but for my ragged sobs and Torren's fading breaths. I crawled to his side, clutching his massive hand in both of mine. amber eyes, dimming, found my own.

"You...fight like...a dragon," he rasped, the barest curl of fanged smile touching his bloody lips. Weak and exhausted from the fight, and losing blood by the minute, he fell into unconsciousness. I held my head up and screamed – giving it every emotion I had – everything I had to give. Everyone stopped abruptly, turning their attention on me, hovering over Torren. My enemies would pay in blood for what they had done.

I stood staring out at the clan. Their pale worn faces looked back at me, lost for words.

"Am I enough for your alpha now?" I demanded. Then proceeded to wipe the blood from my face with distain. "Did I spill enough blood?"

The clan mumbled incoherently, looking around. Their view was clear, there would be no more debate of their loyalty. I was one of them. "Take him to the medical ward, before he bleeds out," I demanded, my tone threatening them to refuse if they dared. Thankfully, they did not, and immediately jumped into action.

The battle was over, but the wounds ran deep. I helped the dragons carry Torren and the injured dragons to the keep's medical ward. Though exhaustion pulled at my limbs, seeing to their care took priority.

Dregan looked on gravely as we worked. "The hoard's divisions may yet cost us all."

I cleaned gashes and bound fractures alongside the healer, a dragon named Adara. Her skill with herbs matched my human medicine. As we tended Ragar's broken wing, he gazed at me thoughtfully but said nothing.

When the last wounds were dressed, Adara saw to mixing potions for the pain. I sank onto a cot, spent both physically and emotionally. The clash of claws and flames replayed in my mind's eye - violence bred more violence, an endless cycle humanity knew all too well.

Torren's voice interrupted my brooding. "Maxine." He was finally awake, and undergoing a blood transfusion. I looked down at him on the bed, smiling sadly. "It looks like they're finally falling into command," he chuckled. I nodded, but said nothing.

I followed wearily to the great hall, where clan members gathered tensely around the edges. Torren stood before the fireplace, looking every inch the authoritative leader despite dust and scratches marring his armour.

Days passed, spending every waking hour by Torren's bedside as he healed. The clan had come to the room for frequent updates on what was going on – and in turn, I gave them updates on Torren's progress. Then, on the eve of the full moon, he was finally discharged from the ward and allowed to go home. He wasted no time in standing before his clan, as they eagerly listened to what he had to say.

"Last week, we discovered new threats within our own ranks," he began gravelly. "Dissent and treachery will not be tolerated. From this moment, any found conspiring against clan interests will face exile...or worse."

Mutterings rippled through the gathering, but none dared argue. Satisfied he'd made his position clear, Torren continued, "Change comes whether we will it or not. Our kind has not mixed with humans in living memory – and it still has not. Maxine, my mate, is a dragon, just like the rest of us."

He gestured to me. Heart in my throat, I stepped forward bravely though uncertainty twisted my insides. All eyes fixed upon me with a thousand judgements dancing behind them.

"This female risked life and limb fighting at our sides today," Torren stated. "By ancient law, she has earned the right to call herself one of us if she wishes. But first, the decision rests with the clan."

The declaration sent shockwaves through my whole being. To finally be accepted after so long struggling against indifference and malice...I dared not let hope take hold just yet. My future hung by a thread in the hands of those who had only known me as enemy.

Ragar was the first to speak, his voice still rough from injury but carrying sincerity. "We have all witnessed her courage and skill. She stood against even our strongest without faltering. Any who rejects her is a fool."

Celise bristled but held her tongue, outnumbered now without her scheming allies. Others voiced agreement gradually, until a consensus formed around me like a shield. The last to weigh in was Dregan, whose solemn affirmation sealed my fate.

By the elders' laws, I was clan.

Tears stung my eyes as relieved laughter and approving cries filled the hall. I let it wash over me like a benediction, releasing the tension wound tight within for so long. Ruthlessly dividing lines blurred into acceptance, if not full understanding yet. But it was a start.

When the noise died down, I met each pair of eyes in turn. "I know the road to true trust is long. But I hope in time, you will see as I have learned to - that underneath our superficial differences, we all wish for safety, purpose and community. Let that be the foundation we build upon going forward."

My words resonated in the echoing spaces, leaving an impression I hoped would endure the tests still to come. Change starts within each individual heart first before rippling outward. That gave me hope our clanship, though born of hardship, could deepen into something meaningful for all.

The days flowed into one another as I settled into clan life. Adara tutored me in herbalism while Dregan instructed me in combat, pushing my limits but with new respect. Nights were spent in the great hall, swapping stories and jokes around the roaring fire as equals.

Being accepted lifted a crushing weight, revealing hidden depths of camaraderie underneath gruff exteriors. Laughter came easier, as did opening up about hopes and losses that transcended species. There was healing to be found in our shared experiences of love, loyalty and perseverance against all odds.

Most surprising was Ragar's blossoming friendship. His surliness melted away into playful banter and long philosophical debates. From him I learned our true nature was far more complex than surface actions alone could every portray. Each being contained multitudes, capable of both great darkness and light.

Only Torren remained an enigma, keeping polite distance as leader though watching me often from his high-backed chair. But one night, as dusk's long shadows dispersed the gathering to their rest, he requested my company in his solar.

Heart thrumming, I followed and took a seat by the fire. A long silence stretched between us before he finally spoke, words tinged with new vulnerability. "You have changed all I once believed of your kind. You seemed destined to disrupt the order...yet brought only healing in your wake. For that, you have my gratitude."

I smiled softly. "Change is never easy, but together we found a better way. Our differences need not divide if we make room for understanding instead."

Something flickered behind his guarded eyes, some acknowledgment of deeper truths left unspoken. And in that moment, I sensed the first fragile vines of trust taking root between dragon and human - a sign of hope that reconciliation was indeed possible, even between old enemies, if one was willing to see with eyes of compassion.

Chapter 16

The medical ward was located deep within the stone fortress, far from the bustle of the great hall and other communal areas. High narrow windows let in sparse natural light, so the long chamber remained dim even during the daylit hours.

I trailed my fingers along the rough-hewed stone walls as I made my nightly rounds, checking on patients from the recent skirmish. Most were sleeping peacefully thanks to Adara's healing arts. Her skills with herbs and poultices far surpassed my own rudimentary medical training, and I admired her patience as a teacher.

The wizened healer currently sat by Ragar's cot, redressing the wound on his massive wing where he'd taken a Warhammer blow. The membrane was knitting cleanly under her ministrations but would still take time to fully mend.

Ragar grunted softly as she applied a pungent salve. "My thanks, Adara. Your arts never fail to amaze this old soldier."

She smiled, eyes crinkling at the corners. "Flattery will get you nowhere, shifter. Now hold still while I wrap this clean."

I lingered to observe, soaking up any knowledge I could. As the last bandage was tied off, I checked Ragar for signs of fever or infection. His forehead felt cool and dry beneath my palm.

"You're progressing well. With continued rest, I expect - "

A groan from the next cot cut me off mid-sentence. Jerking my head around, I realized with dread who the noises were coming from - they weren't ones of pain, but of pleasure and need.

Celise lay in the throes of her yearly heat, tail thrashing the furs as her whimpers grew louder and more animalistic. Liquid amber eyes locked onto mine with pure unreasoning desire, nostrils flaring to take in my scent.

"Please, I need..." she gasped, parting claws with feline grace to reveal glistening pink flesh beneath. An open invitation to any male within vicinity, her body's way of ensuring propagation of their endangered kind.

But all it stirred in me was discomfort and worry for her state of mind. These moments were private affairs for dragons, not to be intruded upon. Yet she didn't seem to comprehend that in her frenzied state, tail coiling sensually along bare limbs.

Before I could react, another voice boomed authoritatively through the chamber. "Cease this at once, Celise."

Torren strode into view, eyes twin flames of dominance and command that rendered her pliant as putty instantly. Her limbs fell still, though arousal still hazed gold irises with primal urges begging fulfillment.

"You embarrass yourself," Torren rumbled darkly. "Control your baser nature as befits your station. There are patients attempting recovery here."

Cowed by her alpha's tone though desperately needing, Celise rolled onto her side with a whimper, curling in on herself protectively. Torren nodded in approval then turned to address me in softer tenor.

"This fire is part of our nature, as inevitable as the tides. See that she is given privacy to ride it out with dignity. The influence of the moon affects us all."

His compassion surprised me, seeing past her wanton display to recognize a biological impulse beyond her control. That depth of understanding between leader and subject heartened me deeply in its own quiet way.

I assured him softly, "She'll come to no harm. Your faith in us is not misplaced."

Torren's mouth quirked upwards almost imperceptibly before striding back out. Order restored, I ushered concerned patients back to their beds while Adara fetched cool compresses. With their help, we settled Celise into a private cell down the hall to ride out the rest of her urges safely away from distressing stimulation.

The next evening found me giving Ragar's wound another once-over by the firelight. His accelerated healing continued to impress, fine black scales already emerging beneath new pink flesh.

"I must thank you for your care, healer," Ragar rumbled in his gravelly baritone once finished. "Few of your kind would show such mercy to enemies."

I smiled gently while packing away my supplies. "We've evolved past enemies, haven't we? Now we seek only to understand one another."

Ragar made a rumbling sound of agreement, thoughtful amber eyes regarding me with new depth. In that comfortable silence, I sensed an invitation for further openness, a willingness to know me as I now knew him - scarred but strong, prideful yet learning compassion runs deeper.

"We all have moments in our past we aren't proud of," he rumbled sagely. "What defines us is how we rise above and grow wiser for the struggle. You have proven tenacity of soul beyond what most ever know."

His words warmed me deeper than the crackling fire ever could. In baring old scars and seeing only understanding in response, walls crumbled further between us, revealing truer friends emerging on the ashes. Our shared experiences of battling inner demons to become more than basal instincts had forged an unbreakable bond.

In the coming nights, other clan members slowly opened up as well, sharing victories and regrets, triumphs and traumas that made them who they were beneath gruff shells. I listened without judgment as they had for me, and found our kinship growing roots deeper than any blood ties could ever compete with. We were a family, chosen and persevering together against all odds.

In the medical ward, Celise's heat finally passed without further incident. Her usual sharp tongue remained restrained as she conveyed gratitude through gracious nods alone. Even surly Dregan dropped by occasionally with curt inquiries into patients' welfare, though keen eyes gave away deeper cares for clan wellbeing.

With each interaction, walls crumbled further as understanding took root where animosity once flourished unchecked. Our differences became less a dividing line and more a bridge to walk together, seeing common hopes in each other our superficial shells once concealed.

This clan was becoming my home, these dragons my family, in all the ways that truly mattered. And I knew with a blossoming hope in my heart, that wherever the winding path ahead might lead, we would walk it side by side, stronger for embracing each other fully as equals with nothing left to prove.

With order restored in the medical ward, I took my leave to seek fresh air in the castle courtyard. The brisk night winds helped clear lingering cobwebs from busy mind and soul.

As I gazed skyward, taking in glittering expanses untainted by human lights, movement caught my eye. Massive shadows wheeled overhead on leathery wings, silhouetted against the stars. Patrols, no doubt, ensuring no further threats lurked beyond the walls this eventful night.

Finishing my contemplations, I then set about assessing damages from our recent skirmish. Much work remained to fortify defences and mend cracked stones where flailing tails had struck with crushing force.

The outer perimeter showed worst depredations. Chunks of crenelations laid shattered where hulking forms collided. Scarred flagstones hinted at spilled blood now washed away by rains.

Claw marks gauged the outer wall where some last stand was mounted against overwhelming odds.

Sighing, I rolled up sleeves and got to work sorting rubble. My lighter strength could at least clear debris for the stronger shifters to lift into place come morning. Methodically I tossed chunks of masonry into growing piles under waning moonlight.

Footsteps alerting me to another's presence, I glanced up to find Torren surveying the ruins as well. His stern profile showed weariness, bearing the weight of command even in private moments. A leader's burdens were never fully shed, it seemed.

We worked in companionable silence for some time, finding camaraderie in shared industry. At length Torren rumbled, "Your efforts have not gone unnoticed. Change was needed, and you brought it with steady hand."

I smiled softly. "We all played our part. Together we've begun to overcome past harms through trust and understanding."

Torren gazed into the distance, eyes alight with some vision I think few if any ever saw. "Aye. Our clan is strongest when we walk as one. You have reminded us what true unity can accomplish, against any force that would see dragons divided."

Warmth bloomed in my chest at his praise, given so rarely but meaning all the more for its sparing nature. We had come far indeed, from the days of tension and fear, to forging bonds that would endure whatever trials the future held in store. This clan was my family now, and I would stand with them always.

The last of the rubble was cleared just as the moon reached its peak in the dark sky. Exhaustion weighed heavily on us after the long day of emotions and labour.

Torren dismissed the other dragons still milling about, sensing our talk was not yet done. He turned to me, amber eyes glinting in the torchlight. "You have challenged all I once knew. Shown me that strength comes too in compassion."

My throat tightened at his uncommon openness. "We all hold prejudices until faced with truth. I'm just happy I could help bridge our community and made us stronger as a whole."

Callused fingers reached out to gently cup my chin, tilting my face up to meet his piercing gaze. Torren had never shown such tender intimacy before, and it stole my breath.

"You brought more than understanding - you awakened what lay dormant in my soul. Showed me life holds beauty still, if only one is willing to see."

Before I could react, his lips captured mine in a lingering kiss that left me trembling from head to toe. All the words left unsaid throughout our journey together poured forth in that searing moment of connection.

When at last we parted, unshed tears shone bright in his eyes. "Stay by my side, little one. Help me lead our clan to new heights of hope and peace."

Joy and wonder welled up inside me until I thought my heart might burst. Throwing my arms around Torren's broad shoulders, I buried my face against his neck with a watery laugh.

"There is no place I would rather be."

And with that, the final walls of mistrust crumbled between us. A new dawn was rising for dragon and human to walk as one.

Chapter 17

The evening sky glowed in shades of purple and orange as rows of torchlight flickered on along the edges of the courtyard. Word had spread far and wide about the celebrations taking place at the fortress that night, and everyone who called this place their home had returned to join in the festivities.

I stood beside Torren near the towering oak doors, nervously adjusting the elegant robes Adara had crafted specifically for this ceremony. "Are you sure about this?" I asked him softly. "Taking on a leadership role is a big responsibility."

He chuckled, the low rumble of his laugh warming me from the inside. "Have faith, my dear. With you by my side, our clan will know a prosperity and peace that until now were only dreams."

Just then, the sound of trumpets echoed through the courtyard, signalling that it was time to begin. Torren swung the heavy doors open with a booming voice, "Let the rites commence!"

We proceeded down the torchlit aisle as dragons and humans alike parted to clear a path for us. Smiles and cheers followed in our wake, filling me with pride for all we had accomplished together through promoting compassion and understanding.

At the end of the walkway sat the clan elders upon an elevated platform, with Dregan and Ragar among their ranks. The veteran warriors grinned cheekily like children awaiting their birthday feast, letting out loud whistles and whoops as Torren and I ascended the steps.

Dregan let out a booming laugh. "Get on with it already, you sentimental lizards! This ale isn't going to drink itself."

Following a chorus of approving hoots and hollers, Ragar then rose to his full imposing height, his rumbling voice carrying across the assembled crowd like rolling thunder. "Clan members, we have gathered here tonight to celebrate new beginnings. With Torren as our stalwart Alpha and young Maxine by his side as our Luna, a new era is dawning for our people!"

His words were met with wild applause and cheers. I spotted Celise beaming up front, her flushed cheeks displaying pride rather than inebriation at long last finding acceptance among the pack. Her growing trust and gentle ways warmed my heart most of all in that moment.

Once the elders' blessings were complete, the official ceremonies came to an end. Torren and I joined in the celebrations alongside everyone else. Dragon and human alike danced together around crackling bonfires as old tales were swapped and hopes voiced for our adventures still to come. Even the usually stern Torren allowed himself to sing heartily, his bass rumble joining in songs of valor and mirth.

Later as the moon rose high in the sky and rounds of ale continued flowing freely, Ragar sidled up to me with a playful glint in his eye. "Not much for idle partying, are you little scholar? Come, I've something to show that ever-curious mind of yours."

He led me up atop the battlements overlooking the forest below, its midnight stretches now aglow with radiant starlight. On the distant horizon, shadows danced upon the inky canvas of the night sky.

Ragar spoke in hushed reverent tones. "My kin have come to pay tribute. It is said to be an omen of prosperity when the wild dragons gather thus to honor new leadership."

Awed, I nestled against his massive side as we watched ancient beings of sky and wood celebrate the blossoming of new life where once had lain only cold stone. Peace, it seemed, had taken root here to stay.

My heart swelled near to bursting at all we had accomplished through spreading compassion. This clan, these dragons - they were truly my family. And together, nothing could stand against the hope and understanding we had won against darkness' deepest tides.

As the celebrations reached their crescendo, an odd sense of unease crept over me that I couldn't seem to shake. Slipping away unnoticed, I made my way through shadowy corridors until reaching the outer walls. There, a flicker of motion along the battlements had caught my attention - a shadow slipping out through the rear gates under cover of night.

My heart began to pound as I hastened down the winding staircase two steps at a time, emerging into the moonlit fields beyond. Scanning the edges urgently, I spotted a figure moving swiftly towards the forest line, billowing skirts catching the breeze. Though features blurred by distance, some inner sense told me with dread certainty who it was.

"Mother, wait!" I cried, breaking into a sprint after her retreating form. Her pace increased at my call, as if pulled by a force beyond will or reason. The thrall of the tree line was calling her away for a final time.

Trees swallowed her up just as I reached the forest edge. Pushing into the murky wood without hesitation, I followed the trailing fabric ever deeper into the realm of night. Vines and gnarled roots snatched at clinging layers, but still I gave chase.

This forest held no fear for me anymore. Its denizens were my kin and I their Luna, destined to protect all children of leaf and claw. My mother would be no exception, not while life yet animated this flesh of hers.

Her form seemed to glide ahead like mist, dancing just out of reach down the slightest of trails. An eldritch quality now suffused glade and thicket awash in ghostly flickering lights between towering sentinels.

A sound suddenly pierced the eerie wood - a keening voice raised in uncanny rapture or agony, impossible now to discern which. It led me onwards to a small clearing awash in silver moon glow.

At its heart stood my mother, head thrown back as fluttering lights writhed around her form. Their whispering voices carried unearthly sweetness yet hinted at veiled mysteries no mortal was meant to grasp.

She turned then with a chilling smile, eyes rolling white as birch leaves rustled around us. A cold laughter spilled forth that chilled me to my core, yet bore no malice - only wild unknowable joy.

With final parting words carried aloft on the breeze - "The dance is nearly done, my child. Soon you too shall understand" - she melted back into the glade without a trace.

I stood frozen, piecing together what had transpired with dawning horror. This wood held darker entities than any mere dragon or wolf, whose magic worked in ways beyond science's ken. My mother had long danced to their fey piping, slipping her mortal bonds when the moon was high.

Now it seemed even I, for all the wonder wrought during this eventful turning, was but a player in deeper mysteries still unfolding. Shivering, I fled the forest's fey heart, seeking refuge once more within stone walls where torchlight kept darker powers at bay.

But some doors, it seemed, were not so easily closed once opened - not against fanciful things that go bump in the night. My journey was far from over, it seemed, in a realm where magic yet worked beyond all mortal reckoning. And in the glade's heart, the dance would continue as it always had, in mysteries no mortal was meant to grasp.

The celebrations at the fortress showed no signs of winding down as midnight drew ever closer. Dragons and humans continued dancing and feasting together, basking in the warm glow of torchlight and good company.

I watched on from my seat beside Torren, contentedness warming my spirit. All the struggles we had endured to build this peace were reflected in each embrace and lively conversation across the crowded courtyard. This clan truly felt like family - it was all I had ever wanted for my adopted people.

As another rousing song rose up accompanied by stomping feet and drums, I happily joined in clapping along to the infectious rhythm. Yet partway through the chorus, an odd sensation arose deep in the pit of my stomach.

Nausea swept over me suddenly, taking me by surprise. I grabbed Torren's massive arm for support as a wave of dizziness threatened to overwhelm. He looked down with concern creasing his strong brow.

"My dear, are you feeling unwell? Perhaps the evening's spirits are not agreeing with you."

I took a steadying breath, about to reassure him it was nothing, when another strange feeling made itself known. My abdomen felt strangely weighted and sensitive to even the lightest pressure.

Memories surfaced of long ago conversations with village midwives, the pieces falling together with startling clarity. My moon cycle had been unusually late, had they not? Could I be...?

Eyes widening, I grasped Torren's massive hand urgently and pressed it against my still-flat stomach. "I think - I believe I may be pregnant."

Shock suffused his noble features as understanding dawned, his gaze shifting between my earnest expression and where his callused palm now rested protectively. A multitude of emotions danced beneath the surface before wonderment took precedence.

"Pregnant?" he gasped, his wide eyes darted to my stomach. "Are you sure?"

I nodded. "I'm quite late. I'm almost certain of it."

He leapt towards the door, his feet skidding across the flooring as he called out as loud as he could muster. "I'm going to be a father!"

Dregan and Ragar were the first to bound over, sweeping us both up in bone-crushing hugs despite Torren's half-hearted protests to mind my condition.

"By the Elder One, I knew this meddling was worth every hassle in the end!" Dregan boomed, thumping our backs heartily.

Ragar managed a gentle smile and rumble, "Our well-wishes go with you both. I'm sure your pup will be as strong as defiantly stubborn as its parents."

Tears of bliss blurred my vision as friend after clan member gathered round to offer heartfelt congratulations and blessings upon our expanding family. In that moment surrounded by grinning faces aglow with good cheer, my heart swelled with certainty that this truly was where I belonged - with this clan, by Torren's side.

Whatever challenges may await in the moons still to come, I knew with calm assurance we would face them united as we had all else. A bright new chapter was unfolding, and I felt ready to walk whatever path it may lead with Torren at my side, our future secure in ways I'd never dreamed that fateful night I first gazed upon these walls.

The promise of compassion we'd fought so hard to cultivate was blossoming fully into being at long last. Peace, joy and understanding had taken root for all our people, both clawed and mortal. Nothing could shake the hope that realization filled me with.

More cheers rose up then as Ragar called for another round of ale to toast the new life growing within the Luna. I laughed and accepted a stone mug, although the heady brew held little appeal now. Torren rumbled softly as he guided me to sit, ever watchful as festivities continued in full swing around us.

A familiar figure soon broke from the jubilant crowd, eyes alight with gentle affection. "Maxine, how wonderful!" Celise beamed, grasping my hands. "May the child know only your kind ways, as you've shown even us scaled ones what it means to walk as one."

Her changed demeanour from our first meeting still moved me deeply. I nodded, smiling. "And may they know the joy you now feel among pack, dear friend. Our paths have taught each well - there is room in this world for all kinds, if we make the choice to understand."

Our conversation flowed on amid cheerful noise and dance, catching each other up on changes since last we spoke at length. Celise spoke hopefully of plans to raise her own young here soon, content as any in finding place and purpose within these walls.

My heart rejoiced to see how far we'd all come. Though mysteries lingered in wood and glade beyond understanding, here was light and love and family - all that truly mattered as life blossomed within and without. This clan would face whatever future may hold, together as one.

The celebration showed no sign of ending as midnight passed into the soft grey light of early dawn. But I soon found myself succumbing to a long awaited sleep, swept into Torren's strong arms and carried gently within the fortress walls. Laughter and song followed even in dreams, carrying fondly the joy of all we'd overcome to find such hope and peace at last.

As I followed the elder deeper into the castle corridors, I gazed upon the intricate stone carvings that lined the walls. Depicted in vivid detail were tales from the clan's ancient history.

I was drawn to one carving showing winged silhouettes against an auroral dawn. "This marks our ancestors' ascension to the skies as guardians," the elder explained.

His words echoed the meaning I sensed in the carvings - a duty to safeguard nature's balance, not assert sovereignty. I realized how limited my initial understanding of this clan had been.

Floating lanterns illuminated our way with a mystical glow. Their flames danced in hues of purple and blue, as beautiful as the night sky. Runes along the frames hinted at spells for continual growth and renewal, reflecting the dragons' reverence for such things.

Each achievement portrayed was not a show of dominance, but an acknowledgment of our interconnectivity with natural forces. Through cooperation, not conquest, challenges were overcome, and knowledge passed to future generations.

As I took in the majestic carvings and profound wisdoms shared, I felt my preconceptions slowly dissolving. This was a civilization deeply spiritual, attuned to forces beyond possession. Here I sensed mysteries that could transform my understanding of humanity itself. I was keen to uncover more of what this place held.

Epilogue

As the first rays of the morning sun kissed the mountain peaks, casting a golden hue over the dragon clan's abode, I stirred from my sleep. I felt the warmth of Torren's presence beside me, his steady breathing a comforting rhythm that echoed the calm strength anchoring our little family. The newborn nestled between us, emitting soft coos that serenaded the dawn.

But duty, as always, beckoned from the realm of dreams and newfound joy. Torren, ever the protector and guide of their people, stirred as I prepared to rise. His gaze, sharp and wise, met mine with unwavering trust.

"Go greet them in peace, as you've always done," Torren murmured, his voice a soothing balm to my worries. "I'll see to our defences and our little one."

My heart swelled with gratitude for his trust, eclipsing the faint tendrils of anxiety that coiled within her. With a tender nuzzle to our infant's little cheek and a whispered promise of a swift return, I hastened towards the Gates.

The news from the guards had stirred murmurs of concern, whispers that danced on the edge of fear. Yet, bolstered by Torren's unwavering faith, I held my head high and my heart open. I stood at the Gates, facing a ragged group that approached our stronghold.

The leader, an elderly woman with weathered lines etched upon her face, dismounted from her weary steed with a stiffness that bespoke a lifetime of hardship. Her eyes, though tired, held a glimmer of resilience that sparked something deep within my chest.

"We seek refuge," the woman's voice trembled with the weight of sorrow and desperation. "Raiders razed our village; we've nowhere else to turn."

Compassion swelled within my heart, the same empathy that had once welcomed her into the embrace of this clan when she was an outsider. I reached out, clasping the weary hands of the elder in hers.

"Here, within our lands, you'll find solace and sanctuary," I spoke with a conviction that echoed across the clearing. "Come on in."

The gates swung open, revealing the unfamiliar faces, wearied and apprehensive, peering up at the towering fastness of the Dragon clan's home. Slowly, the outsiders were welcomed in, greeted not with suspicion but with open arms and genuine curiosity.

Amidst the bustle of the newcomers settling in, Maxine and Torren found themselves juggling their roles as leaders, parents, and compassionate hosts. Balancing the needs of their people with the demands of parenthood was a delicate dance, one that required patience, understanding, and a shared commitment.

Their interactions with the newcomers mirrored the spirit of unity that the Dragon clan embodied. The younglings darted ahead, extending innocent gestures of aid, while the elders brought provisions and offered healing remedies, bridging the gap between the two groups.

As days turned into weeks, the once cautious glances between the clans softened into genuine camaraderie. Ryon, once guarded and aloof, found common ground with some of the newcomers, forming unexpected friendships that blossomed amidst shared stories and moments of vulnerability.

Amidst our duties, stole precious moments with their little one, watching in wonder as the baby grew and thrived in the embrace of their loving clan.

The bond between the two groups strengthened, nurtured by shared experiences and a common desire for peace and understanding. The Dragon clan and the newcomers became intertwined, their lives weaving together like threads in a rich tapestry, each contributing to the other's story.

In this remote mountain fastness, where dragons soared overhead and kindred spirits found solace, the winds of change whispered tales of unity, resilience, and the unyielding power of compassion.

Enjoyed the book?

Please take five minutes to let the readers know what you thought of this book.
It might not seem like much, but I rely on reviews for my book to be seen.

About the Publisher

FaeDream Publishing is a brand-new publishing house focusing on the Paranormal Shifter Romance.
We have been setting up for a couple of years, making sure we have everything in place before launching our books and accepting submissions.
Now open, in 2024, we can't wait to go on this amazing journey with both our writers and our readers!

Website
https://faedreampublishingbooks.wordpress.com
YouTube Channel
https://youtube.com/@faeDreamPublishing
Newsletter Signup
https://subscribepage.io/gT88PJ

Printed in Great Britain
by Amazon